FEATHER

Evan Benner

Printed in the United States of America

First Printing, 2017

ISBN 978-0-692-87895-8

Benner Books
5904 Corte Espada
Pleasanton, CA 94566

Dedicated to Doctor Tompkins and to Jackson

BRING ME ALONG

That guy Feather, he was one hell of a dude. First time I met him, back in 2016, was by complete chance. My buddy Drew and I had drove up from Santa Cruz to the Shoreline Amphitheater to catch a Dead and Company show. We'd spent the past week traveling north from San Diego in my godfather Skip's van with our boards, hitting every solid spot we could find. We were stopping here before turning around and heading back south, all the way to Baja to stay with my aunt.

I was the first to see him, clean cut hair and a bit of scruff on his face with one hell of a little blondie with him, Laura. He was tall and lean with this wild look in his eyes, I could instantly tell he was different than all the other people Drew and I had met on our road trip. Something told me I had to introduce myself to this guy, this stranger over there was the key. Key to what, I had no idea at the time, but he was definitely the key to something kickass, something wild, something that changed my entire life.

That guy Feather had a surfboard just sitting on top of his car, and he was about to leave it sitting in a parking lot! I ran up to him and yelled, "Hey dude! Somebody is gonna swoop your surfboard! Do you wanna put it in my van until this show is over?"

"How do I know you won't just take my stick?" he answered.

"Well, you don't, but trust me I won't!"

"Ah shit why not, Laura chill here for a minute I'm gonna put my board in this guy's car. What's your name, man?" Feather asked, his voice a bit raspy, not really low, but not real high, this cool in between. He spoke slow for a Californian, but it was because he really drew out each word, took time to really feel each word he said, despite it's importance. No matter what he said, he made it something worth saying, even if it was total nonsense, but it didn't matter because you could listen to anything this guy said. It wasn't like he had a beautiful voice like Morgan Freeman's, but there was just something about the way he talked, he really put something else into everything he said that made each sound coming out of his mouth like its own little song.

"My names Kevin, this is Drew, who are you?" I asked.

"Name's Ethan Feather, but most just call me Feather," he replied.

"Good to meet you Feather, you can just throw your board in here, you from around here?"

"Ya, over by Berkeley, I'm out going down the coast with my friend Lauralyn over there, we're taking a little road trip down to Encinitas by San Diego to see my cousin and surf. She never has and I thought this would be a good time to teach her. Kickin it off here with a nice little trip and the Dead, no better way to start a road trip."

"I know where Encinitas is! Drew and I are down from San Diego and we've been hitting every break along the coast. We're headed back down south after this to go chill in Baja, you should come down after you see your cousin!"

2

"I might just take you up on your offer, but I need to know if I like you enough or not, come trip with us!" Feather said as I opened the van to reveal mine and Drew's 5 boards sitting in there. I'd never done anything more than smoke pot a couple times, so this offer of doing LSD was a bit intimidating and I was ready to turn down the offer, but just like the feeling I felt when I first saw Ethan, I knew I had to do this.

"I've never tripped before, but what better place to do it than here! You in Drew?" I said.

"Why the hell not, I did this back when we went senior camping, and it was pretty cool," Drew cooly answered. Drew was short with black hair with blonde streaks from saltwater and sunshine, half Korean, half Filipino. Back at school he was known as pretty crazy and was my polar opposite in almost every way other than our shared love of surfing and similar music tastes. He spoke fast and was a true southern Californian, fit every stereotype perfectly even though he'd lived in Florida for the first 13 years of his life. Whenever I got into trouble, he was normally the one talking me into doing whatever it was getting me in trouble, whether it was tagging, trespassing, or other nefarious no-good things he was so fond of.

"Grate! Follow me, Laura has all the stuff, she's right over there," Feather said and we followed.

We went over behind some porta-potties in the parking lot and there was that blonde girl I'd seen a bit ago, and she was smoking one of the thickest joints I'd seen in my life. Something about the way she just stood there, leaning a bit to the left with this carefree, loving look in her eyes. She looked younger than Feather who I knew was younger than myself and Drew, and we just turned 19 two days go (our birthdays were on the same day, which was the only reason we even became friends in the first place). But back to Laura, that first time I saw her, I'm always gonna remember that moment. When I first looked at her it was like looking at something out of a dream and all I did was silently pray to whatever, god, gods, goddesses, or all-powerful force controlled the universe that she was single.

"Break out the acid, Laura, we're popping this kids trip cherry!" Feather said with this huge grin on his face.

Laura smiled at me and handed me this little orange gel tablet containing 150 micrograms of LSD, more than enough to open my eye to that new world I'd later hear Feather talk about all the time, and more than enough I'd need to trip through the whole dead show. I'd heard about bad trips before, but for some reason I felt really comfortable with these complete strangers. I felt really happy every time I'd look at Laura and to this day, anything Feather said I'd do without question because I knew in the end it'd all turn out alright because he was just that kinda guy.

All of the sudden this seemingly carefree guy, the kind of guy who, even if a gun was pointed to his head would crack a dick joke, this carefree guy suddenly got serious for a minute. He put his hand on my shoulder and looked me straight in the eyes and I could see what he was about to say was something he honestly and truly believed.

"What's about to happen is, well, you're not just gonna get high, you're gonna trip. There's no way to actually describe tripping, words can't possibly come close to describing a trip. This little bit of psychedelic psubstance here is about to open your eyes to a whole

4

new world, let you really see yourself and who you are. MY goal, my goal, is for someday, someday for you and I and Drew and Laura and everybody all to be able to have our eyes open to this, but not because we're tripping. I want people to do these drugs until they don't need to do them anymore. This author dude, Alan Watts, once said psychedelic drugs are like getting a phone call, but once you get the message, you hang up. That's what I want for us. I want us to get that message, and I want everybody to get that message. I honestly believe if that happens, we're gonna have peace. People are gonna stop dying for no reason in wars that nobody has any business fighting, people are gonna stop hating people we have no business hating, and people are just gonna be people!" Feather explained, and in that moment, all my fears of dropping acid vanished and were replaced by this feeling of excitement for whatever adventure the next eight hours were about to be. Well, I thought it would only be eight hours, but in a few weeks I was about to learn that the trip was going to last a lot longer than that.

"Feather, shut your hippy mouth and just let the guy trip!" Laura exclaimed laughing. We all joined in, creating a beautiful symphony of laughs, each with our own distinct sound that perfectly melded together.

I pulled my long, nearly shoulder-length hair back into a pony tail that excluded the back of my hair, kind of like what samurai used to do, and I put that tablet under my tongue and let it melt. It took a bit for it to dissolve and a bit more for it to start to kick in. It just crept up on me, real slow-like, and then it pounced, similar to the way a mountain lion would jump on its prey. Colors got brighter and were more defined, everything was more defined, hell I could see the cells

in the grass I was walking on with my barefeet! Wait...
shit I was barefoot! Where'd my shoes go? Where'd
my shoes go I don't have any shoes! Where the hell'd
my shoes go! I turned to Laura because I knew she'd
have the answers to my problems because goddammit
she was amazing, even though I'd known her for an
hour she definitely was. Where the hell are my shoes?

"Laura! Where the hell are my shoes!" I
demanded. I had to know, I had to know where the hell
my shoes were!

"Kevin... you haven't had shoes this whole
time. I think it hit him guys," she said and laughed that
lovely laugh.

"Kevin you haven't had shoes since we surfed
Rincon! Remember, you gave them to that homeless
guy so he'd get us a six pack!" Drew said. He looked at
me and I looked at him, his pupils were giant and I
knew mine must have been as well. I looked at Laura
and her's were giant as well, and I grabbed Ethan's
shoulder and looked him right in his eyes, and his
pupils were wide, wide open.

Eyes are the windows to the soul and I knew
then that our pupils were big because those windows
were just blown wide open. I saw right into Feather's
soul and I saw something I couldn't explain. Inside this
man, this kid, this guy a year younger than me I saw a
soul older than everybody in a 100 mile radius put
together. There was something different about this
guy, goddamn Feather. I knew I had to see him in
Baja. I knew I needed to go on an adventure with this
guy, and I knew if Feather had the chance he'd change
the world. Would I ever see him again? Would I see
him in Baja? *FEATHER ARE YOU COMING TO
BAJA? CAN YOU EVEN HEAR ME? HOLY SHIT I'M*

YELLING MY THOUGHTS IN MY HEAD! THIS IS NUTS! Well now I'm whispering how quiet can I get? Okay that's much too quiet. What was I trying to figure out? Oh ya, FEATHER ARE YOU COMING TO BAJA MAN? ETHAN YOU NEED TO COME TO BAJA GODDAMMIT!

Feather grabbed my shoulder just as I was grabbing his. I almost forgot I was still staring into his eyes, but he just looked into me and nodded. I have no idea how, but Feather knew exactly what I was thinking, he could straight read my mind. A bond was made right then and there, one that was about to last a long while. I could tell what he was thinking, I couldn't actually hear his thoughts, but I would always be able to tell exactly what he was thinking, and he would be able to do the same for me.

We got to the gate and the people were checking tickets. Oh god where's my ticket- where's my ticket where's my-

"Ticket." the guard said, hiding his soul behind his dark sunglasses. He should really let more natural light in, it's good for the spirit ya know.

"Ticket sir," he said as I kept walking and realized I had to show him the ticket I couldn't find in my pockets.

"Right here!" I quickly spat out, my normally cool and calm voice cracked and came out quickly, my words tasted awful talking to this guy. I didn't realize it but my ticket was actually in my hands and I'd been worrying about nothing. You know that's something that people do a lot, worry about things they really don't need to worry about, overthinking is a real problem nowadays.

We got inside with no problem and Laura

pulled me aside, laughing. Laughing at what? Was there something on my face? Oh no there was something on my face or in my teeth, or maybe it was my breath. Did my breath smell? Sweet jesus this girl is gorgeous, look at her, the things I-

"Kevin, you are most definitely tripping way to hard. Take a second. Just sit down here on the grass, ya like that, that's good, just look at me, you're good, you're just tripping. Here, I snuck this in, we're gonna smoke it and it's going to chill you out and you're going to have an amazing trip, ok?" Laura explained as she pulled out a tiny joint from her bra and a lighter from her pocket. I don't remember sitting down but I assume I plopped down when she told me to, Drew and Feather continued on to go and watch the Dead start to play.

I watched her spark the lighter to light the joint and everything slowed down. There was a gentle breeze that carried this wonderful, beautiful, calming, happy sound from miles and miles away. No, not miles, it was the band. They started playing Box of Rain just as Laura took the first hit. She exhaled a purple, blue, and red cloud that spiraled up into the sky, up into eternity. It was going on it's way, following the wind, going where the wind takes it. That's when I decided two things. Music was so powerful, it brought joy to people, it spread happiness. That's all I wanted to do in life, make people happy. I also decided:

"I want to just make people happy. Music makes people happy. I want to make music Laura. But I wanna make certain people happy too. I wanna make you happy. Make sure you guys come to Baja, Laura," I said. Somethings in life I've said and I've been sure about, and I was so sure about that, more sure about that than anything else I'd ever said in my whole entire life.

"You're cute you dirty hippy, now take a hit of this, and get some shoes when you get a chance," Laura said and leaned up next to me as I brought the joint to my lips.

I looked down and that little guy smiled back at me, he knew what he would do, he was like me and just wanted to make people happy. I saw a tiny little arm stick out the side and give me a thumbs up as I inhaled and the paper turned orange and pink, then a whole plethora of colors as it diminished while I sucked and sucked. Goddamn I took the biggest hit of my life in that moment, it just felt so good. Normally it felt like tiny pins sticking into my throat and lungs, but this was a warmth, like that of the bonfire from a few nights ago, or how it felt to swallow down freshly speared rockfish that got cooked on a spit... Drew! Laura and I had to go find Feather and Drew! We had to watch the band play!

We finished the joint and I jumped up and grabbed Laura's hand and brought her along through the crowds until we found our friends who were all in their happy places. We got up and put arms around each other's shoulders and just listened to Ripple as it was brought to us on giant colorful waves of this beautiful sound. Sober I always just thought of it as happy music, but now I know it was euphoric. I stood there with my best friend and two people who I'd only met around two hours ago, but I could've known them my whole life and first experienced euphoria. At that time I couldn't explain what it was, later I'd be able to, but in that moment I didn't care I couldn't explain what was going on because it was amazing. This beautiful time didn't need to be explained, it just needed to be

9

experienced.

We were coming down as the show ended, and we just realized we'd been standing the whole time. What also was noticed was it was now nighttime. We were all outside but we were all so wrapped up in that amazing experience we didn't realize the sun had set long ago and the moon had replaced it. All four of us just sat then laid on our backs.

"Do you see the grid? Look, all the stars, it's like a grid!" Drew pointed out. And I did see it, so did Laura, so did Feather.

"Every time, no matter who I'm with, we all always see it. That grid, it let's me know that ya, this is a drug and it's making us trip and hallucinate, but it's also letting us see more. More of the world, more of what's really there. I like you guys, I really do. I don't think I've ever met anybody I like more than you two. Even though there were thousands of people here, I felt like it was only us four, and I've never felt that before, not on any trip," Feather said with his beautiful way of saying things. To this day in that moment, I've never felt more at peace with myself, or with this world, and I knew what I had to ask, but wasn't going to, not yet, I had to wait. Twenty minutes, just twenty more minutes if we laid there I would ask because that would mean the universe wanted it. I don't quite know why I thought the universe would want it or why twenty minutes would mean it did, but that's what I thought so I stuck by it, and, you know what? Those twenty minutes did pass. Twenty whole minutes of stillness, silence, the entire venue had cleared, and eventually it was just us laying on the lawn, motionless, and I asked it.

"So you're coming to Baja?" I asked, breaking the silence, the beautiful silence.

"Of course! Honestly, I would've forgotten if you hadn't asked, but I'll definitely see you there. Laura give Kevin your phone number, I threw my phone in the water when we hit San Francisco after we left last night," Feather answered.

So Laura gave me her phone number and then I shot straight up. I darted off towards the amphitheater and the other three followed me, confused, but they followed. I got to the doors to get in but security was there, barring the only way in. I turned around, disappointed, then Feather darted off and we followed him. I knew he knew what I wanted to do, we were going to go meet Bob, Feather knew the way to get to him. Well, he didn't actually know the way, but he'd find it because he's Feather and that's what Feather does. There was a guy acting up off in the distance, distracting the guard who was inching closer to the stranger and we slipped past him, like shadows, we were in. The stage was empty, but Mickey, Bill, and Bob were still down there, sitting on the edge laughing. The four of us walked towards them, slowly, then faster and faster, but no faster than a brisk walk.

Bob saw us first and pointed us out to the other two who just sat there and watched us approach, calm as could be. I heard a little chuckle as I got closer, I think it was Bill, and they did nothing. Some bands might've called for security, but these guys in their old age didn't care for that, they knew we weren't going for autographs. The old music veterans knew all we wanted was good company for a conversation after a trip, since they've been in that same position.

"Hi, I'm Bob, what's your name?" Weir piped

up first, we all knew who would respond first.

"Ethan, but they call me Feather. This is Lauralyn, but she goes by Laura, that's Drew, but I think I'm gonna start calling him Big D, and this is Kevin, she likes to just call him Dirty Hippy, so I do too," Feather said, casually introducing us to this guy apart of a band I'd worshipped since I was 14.

"What're you guys doing down here?" Mickey asked.

"I dunno, I was just bored, and we all just tripped, and I thought you guys would be cool to talk to," I said, suddenly relaxed after Feather demonstrated that it was easy to talk to these guys. They were just people anyway. We all relaxed and as the final traces of the substance left our minds we began to wrap up our 30 minute conversation with these amazing people, and we all began to leave when I felt something tap my shoulder. It was a finger, and attached to that finger was a hand attached to an arm that was attached to Bob Weir.

"You said it was your first trip, did you realize anything? That first trip has your most important realization, a lot of people miss it though," he asked.

"I don't think I did. I was sitting on the grass with Laura and we were smoking when you guys started to play, my trip was scary at first but your music changed it and made me happy. I realized I wanted to be able to do that, to make people happy," I replied.

"And how do you think you can do that?"

"I'm gonna make music. I can barely play anything but the bongos and a harmonica, but I'm gonna make music that'll make people happy."

"I don't know how, man, but I thought you'd say that. I had the same realization on my first trip. I

12

want you to have this, but you have to swear to me you're going to use it not for the money and the fame, but for making people happy, and yourself happy of course. But you easily could just get rich, but you know, man, you've got to spread your message," Bob said as he handed me a guitar. "Don't worry, I've got around a hundred at home, but I want you to have this."

"Thank you so much, I'll make the best music I can with it," I responded, not knowing what else to say and left to catch up with the other three waiting for me in the parking lot.

"Feather and Laura left. Laura said she'd text you tomor- HOLY SHIT WHERE'D YOU GET THAT!" Drew exclaimed, seeing the guitar I held in my hands.

"You're not going to believe it, but Bob Weir gave it to me. Now I just need to learn how to play it," I explained as I loaded the guitar into the van.

It was late, a bit after midnight, but I wasn't a bit tired so we decided to start our long trek and get as much road behind us as we could. Drew and I were headed to Pescadero, where we could stay with my aunt who lived down there, 1400 miles away. IT was down pretty far south on the peninsula, about an hour north of Cabo and the drive would take about three days without any stops, but damn that's a whole 1400 miles of coast! There's no way there wouldn't be any stops.

I plugged my phone into the aux and Drew fell asleep while I blasted down the highway. Nobody around at this time of night, so I drove as I pleased. There's no feeling that feels more free than the feeling you feel while you're soaring down an empty road to a great playlist. That feeling I felt is something I wouldn't trade to feel any other feeling, not even the feeling felt that day tripping on LSD. Natural euphoria.

The only freedom comparable to driving at such a time at night is that rush of dropping in on a wave that you know you have no business paddling after, much-less trying to ride. Charging down the line on a wave bigger than you are, that power, that speed, that solitude... it's the only thing as good as solid music on an empty road in the middle of the night, the whole world open and nobody there to stop you.

While we're driving down this road, I think it's a good idea to take a break from my story and tell you a bit about myself. My name is Kevin Douglas and I'm a dirty, orphan hippy who could give two shits as long as I get to surf and have a good time (nothing has changed much between then and now). When I was 2 my mom abandoned my dad and I, so she was as good as dead, and then when I was 9 my dad was diagnosed with throat cancer from his chewing habit that took his life 3 years later. I got sent across the country from my house in New York, to a new home in California to live with my dad's best friend growing up: John Franco the third, or Skip. Skip ran a surf shop, shaped his own surfboards, and was dirt poor, but he didn't mind. When I was thirteen I asked him why he was so okay with his financial situation thinking back to the affluent people who the media made seem so important. I still remember it, he looked me right in the eyes with his hand on my shoulder, just like Feather did at the concert and told me "I bet none of those sons of bitches are happy. I wanted to get rich so I could surf, but why not just surf and cut all the stress out?"

The death of my dad was awful, but a blessing

in disguise, because that day I realized I'd been saved from a life I definitely would've loathed, I was meant to be like Skip, and being like skip means being happy and not giving a shit. He started "home-schooling" me after I told him I wanted to learn something important, so he taught me to surf, shape, and spearfish, but most importantly he taught me to be a good person. Skip's religion was the ocean and nothing else, but he loved Jesus and he loved the Buddha. Everyday at breakfast and every night at dinner he'd read me a quote from each and ask me what the quote meant to me before explaining it from his point of view, and then he'd go on to say the best part about not being apart of these two guys' religions was we could each have our own view on what they taught, and neither of us would be "wrong". My favorite reason was the fact without the barrier of actually pledging myself to a religion is I was able to see the similarities between them all, and ultimately seeing how those similarities could all be traced back to a mysterious force, being, energy, or whatever the hell it is that goes by the name of God.

I'd had a couple friends here and there, but they were just the beach bums and the regulars of Skip's shop, nobody who was really my age would spend time with the weird, homeschooled, hippy kid until I was fifteen. This short Asian looking guy charged into me and we both tumbled to the floor on my way from the beach to the shop one day. I heard somebody shout "You two! Stop!" and I knew I had to run with this guy wherever he was going. I hid my speargun and catch in an empty trashcan nearby, and I chased after this random kid, kinda pissed off that now I was running from what I assumed was a cop.

Although restricted by the wetsuit I was half-wearing, I easily caught up to the guy and passed him before vaulting over a low fence and hiding in an old building. This kid quickly entered the same spot as I, and we sat in silence for 20 minutes before we knew it was safe.

"Sorry about that, it was fun though, wasn't it?" the stranger had said.

"Who the hell are you and why were you running?" I exclaimed.

"Name's Andrew but everybody calls me Drew. That cop was just pissed I was gonna smoke this in public again," he said as he pulled out a small, weird-looking cigarette.

"That's a funky stoge, what the hell is that?"

"You mean you've never seen a joint before?"

"Like, a marijuana joint?"

"Hell ya, you wanna smoke it?"

"Why the hell not, I'm Kevin."

In that moment I not only discovered why people smoked pot, but I also met one of my best friends that day. Drew got me into all sorts of trouble all the time, but I honestly didn't care as much as I let on since I just wanted an excuse to give him a hard time. He went to one of the local high schools and was one of the more popular kids, so he got me into parties and social events all the time. Hell, the guy couldn't find me a prom date that would take me, so he wrote in on his ticket that I was his date! We had all kinds of fun together, even more so once I taught him how to surf.

Drew took me to social events and I took him out on the water, we taught each other to be better with each. After Drew graduated he went to community college so we could still hangout, as I was just working the shop with Skip, shaping and surfing all day.

That summer after his first year of college, I thought up of an idea for a nice road trip up and down the coast, hitting every solid spot from Pacifica to Pescadero. It "would only last a couple weeks" so he'd be back in time for college to start. It would turn out it was going to last a lot longer than just a couple weeks, but you'll see that a bit later.

Before I knew it, I was stopped by LA, somewhere near Venice beach, the sun rising over the water as I pounded a monster and waxed my board up to get a couple waves in before Drew took over driving. I sent Laura a text telling her where in Mexico we were headed and where to find us when she got there. I also reminded her to hide the LSD somewhere in the car and to get rid of their weed before they went over the border. Not even Drew was crazy enough to try and bring that over.

I paddled out and the cold water hitting my tired face woke me up a hundred times more than caffeine could. Nobody was out, the waves were solid, and the water was glassy as could be. The first wave I caught was a real nice one, only five feet tall but it broke real nice; not too fast but with enough power behind it to give a real good umph, and that ride was real long. I had no idea what the break was called, I'd just pulled over when I saw the break and headed down to the beach. It didn't need a name, it just needed to be surfed and that's what I was doing. My own form of art, my own way to express what I felt. My long, light brown hair turned black from the water, definitely none of my usual blonde streaks in it this morning as I surfed in an easy and laid-back way, unlike I'd ever surfed before. After seeing the hidden, psychedelic world the night before and truly experiencing euphoria, I was surfing in a way I believe portrayed bliss. There I was, wave after wave, set after set. For about an hour and a half truly I was free, truly in my element, surfing better than I had ever before. Nobody was there to see, but that didn't matter because I did more than just see, I experienced. I felt. That morning I discovered the meaning of transcendence. I was one with the wave, with the ocean. I was one with everything in it, and it was all one with me. Then I packed up, woke up Drew, and told him to go drive somewhere for breakfast.

We got to a Burger King drive-thru and at this point we still had money, so we bought our food and carried on our merry way. I ate more that morning than I think anybody should ever eat in one sitting, and I was still starving, so hungry, but a hunger that would lose to exhaustion, it was time to sleep...

ROSARITO

I woke up and we were in Mexico and Drew was haulin' down the highway. We were still in northern Baja and I knew he didn't want to spend much time here so he was going fast as he legally could to avoid la policia, since local cops here weren't always the most honest, but we still had a little run in. Although he wasn't breaking any traffic laws, Drew got pulled over and we were about to be in a bit of trouble. The officer came up to the van and tried speaking broken English, but Skip taught me enough Spanish to get by and I was able to tell him:

"I'm sorry sir, we'll meet you at the station in town."

"I'll need your license to be sure you're coming."

"No problem here you go!" I said as I handed him an old, expired license that I'd brought along for this exact scenario. The officer headed back to the police station and I instructed Drew to drive and not look back.

"He's got your license dumbass!" Drew exclaimed.

"He's got my old license, now go!" I responded, not wanting to run into more trouble.

The next few hours were pretty uneventful until we caught a glimpse of coast, and I told Drew to pull over. I went in the back and grabbed my binoculars before climbing on top of the Vanagon to get a better look at the stretch of solitude. The beach had beautiful white sand and I could make out waves that, from on top of the van, looked really good. I clambered back in and shouted "Drew drive over to this beach, we're going to surf the hell out of it!"

"We're in the middle of nowhere, are you sure this is safe?" he replied.

"Well, I think we're far enough south that we're gonna be good for a night. Drew, we have to surf this, it didn't look killer, but I know we have to at the very least go down to that beach," I explained.

Drew knew he wouldn't be able to convince me otherwise, not in a million years because I was exactly like him in that once my mind was set on something, there was no changing it. Normally I was open minded, but for certain things, I could put a mule to shame. It took about thirty minutes for us to get down to this tucked away beach on a narrow dirt road that obviously wasn't used very often. We parked the van about fifteen feet from the beach before inspecting the break. The waves were small, around three feet in height, but they broke nice and easily and kept breaking for what could've been miles.

We broke out our longboards and paddled out, noticing a rock reef bustling with activity below us that stretched all along the coast. Before I went to charge my first wave, I saw it, a cabezon, and a big one! I rode this wave all the way into the beach, dancing up and down my board with a grace that came with years of practice. Riding a shortboard and going fast, doing hard turns, huge airs were all fun, but nothing beat the laid back longboard style. It wasn't about who could go the craziest, who could do the most technical move, but whose style was the greatest. Riding a longboard was the greatest way for an individual to express themselves through surfing, it was truly an art. I did what I could to express the pure joy brought by the ocean through my riding. On this board I danced like Feather spoke: gracefully and surely. Goddamn, I couldn't wait to see that kid.

The wave ended after blessing me with a ride that lasted around a minute and a half. I'd never had a ride like that before in my life, but there were also priorities to fun. Drew and I had to eat and we were running low on candy and beef jerky, we needed some actual food in our stomaches this night. I went back to the van and grabbed my speargun and donned my dive gear before swimming back out. It was an easy spot to dive, only about thirty feet, giving me about a minute and a half on the bottom before having to go back up for air.

I plunged down, my long-bladed fins high in the air as I submerge, pinching my nose to equalize my ears, and I was immersed in an entirely new world. This place is alien to most, but after years of doing this almost everyday, it's a second home. There's a certain comfort with being under. My few worries were irrelevant and I'm only focused on a few things, my prey, my breath, and other predators. That's the beautiful thing about spearfishing, you're not just dragging a line through the water, you're actually in it, trying to outsmart the fish so you can eat, you're not just taking from the food chain, you're on the food chain. In the water almost everything is faster and more comfortable than yourself, and you're definitely not on the top of the food chain. Thankfully, we're not fat enough for sharks to really enjoy so most of the time, they let well enough alone, and if they don't, a couple pokes to the nose will get them to fuck off, and if it doesn't, you better be a fast swimmer.

It took about thirty minutes for me to spear my first fish, a good sized cabezon, hiding in a little crevice. I had no clear shot at it between the sharp rocks, but saw light peeking through on the other side. After jamming the tip of my spear into its hole, I grabbed one of the rocks and launched myself to the other side where my dinner was just swimming out. I let it swim a bit before sticking my gun ahead of me and launching my spear at it, and I nailed it! Right in the sweet spot through the spine on the neck, quick and clean. As humane as you can get. Just in case, I took my knife and brained it to make sure it really is dead, and that's when you jam a knife right in the sweet spot. That's when I realized, I'd been down there far too long.

A short, adrenaline-induced trip in the water instantly ended the moment I emerged. I was gasping for air, filling my lungs back up, and stringing my catch. I saw Drew paddling back in and I followed suit, and quickly my feet were on the warm Mexican, white sand. The intro from Hotel California began to play in my head, or was it on some speakers? Oh man, Drew was playing it in the car, he knows what to play and when to play it. We truly were in the Hotel California, the one of Baja California. This is what it really means, on a warm beach, hot sun coming down, and an amazing day on the water. Honestly, that may have well been the best moment of my whole life.

I got back to Drew, I asked if he was gonna eat some of the fish I caught. He quickly agreed and I had him clean it. I passed him the fish and he deftly filleted the savory meat, but due to a lack of salt and pepper (or any spices for that matter), Drew simply took the remaining beef jerky we had and rubbed it until all the seasoning came off on the fish. I threw the slabs of fish on some hot rocks that I had put some saltwater on back when the fire first started. They sizzled and they fizzled, they made their own beautiful song, one that came with an aroma to die for. The scent of the cooking cod was a symphony of its own. The meat was beautifully cooked and it more than satisfied the eyes, and the meat not only tasted like food of the gods, but felt amazing as it slowly but ever so surely melted into my mouth. The warmness of the meal traveled all the way down to my stomach, getting ready to give me energy for the next day, which would include driving, more surfing, and more spearfishing to satiate my remaining sense, which was unsatisfied by a simple meal.

Just as I was taking another bite, I smelt something in the air, something almost completely masked by the smell of dinner. *That smell I smell... it... I think it's weed.* I handed Drew his share of the dinner and spoke up, "Dude, I think I smell weed."

"Kevin, I think I smell it too! But, what if it's like, a buncha cartel dudes? What then?" Drew asked.

"It could be a farm, let's go" I said as I pulled him up from the spot he sat in.

We wandered towards the familiar smell (very familiar, I think Drew might've smoked some while I was out, now that I think back on it), and it just got stronger and stronger, and then, I saw the first row of them. A farm, a farm of weed, this was a gift from the whole goddamn universe. Knowing that this is obviously not something to mess with, we only took a tiny bit, how much you might ask? Exactly about an Irish Wee Bit, or IWB to shorten it. I'd say that the amount in a system that you, the reader, is much more familiar with, would be about four and a half ounces, each. That amounted to nine ounces between the two of us as we headed back to the van. I loved that beach, but we definitely weren't spending the night on it. It proved to be far too close to unwanted trouble.

The deal was for an hour, we'd drive, and the whole time, Drew would roll joints, fatties too, mind you. We were bound to find a beach to stay at, that we wouldn't get murdered or kidnapped at, and it'll be just as awesome as the last. The hour passed quickly with good music and good company and I pulled off the side of the road again and drove on down to a different beach. This one was gorgeous and the sun was almost done setting, so we got the greatest show mother nature could provide: a sunset on an empty ocean from an empty beach. We sat there in the middle of the balance between day and night. The sun and moon matched each other at the equator and, for a brief second, that brief second, everything was at peace and balanced. That moment must happen everyday, but that was the first time I ever truly noticed and observed that moment.

We slept in sleeping bags in the back of the van, using longboards we took fins off of as mattresses. It wasn't the most comfortable, but it was one of the best sleeps I ever had because, we'd enjoyed a bit of the fruits of our labor from the farm. I was just laying when the next song played on the playlist played: The General. One of my favorites for a long time, I listened to the guitar playing in admiration, wishing I could replicate it. I hadn't played guitar for around 7 or 8 years, I'd given up after about 9 months of lessons when I was younger. I decided to get out of my sleeping bag, and pick up the guitar Bob Weir had given me. Still heavily under the influence, I just played what I wanted until I remembered I wanted to play The General. I messed around with the chords and the finger placements, barely knowing what I was doing, and after about an hour, I finally got it. I'd been playing the song on repeat the whole time and on this final and successful attempt, I had played the guitar riffs at the end of the song along with the guitarist on the recording. Promptly after, I realized that I was exhausted again and I climbed back in bed.

I woke in the morning and we were already moving, Drew had started driving while I was still sleeping earlier that morning to make more progress. We were nearing our destination, not too much further until we got to Pescadero. I drove the second half of the day after we refueled from gas tanks we'd brought ourself to make sure we'd get there. The drive felt long and extremely hot and that van just made it take so much longer. That boring, ugly, old VW Vanagon surprisingly held up well. I sat there and contemplated what to do with the old, drab exterior, right up until I pulled into town, driving past a wall of graffiti I knew what we had to do: we could paint it.

I pulled up to my aunt's condo, the place we were to be staying, and walked in. Drew was drowsy as he'd just been woken up from a nap. I knocked, and in a few seconds my aunt opened the door, extremely ecstatic to see I'd finally made it down. She'd expected me a day earlier, but we'd made our stop at the beach to surf so we showed up later than expected.

"What've you been up to lately, man?" she asked.

"Not much, just been surfing a bunch. I went to a Dead and Company concert before coming down here, Drew and I met a cool dude named Feather and his friend Laura. They're visiting Feather's cousin in San Diego and then meeting us down here," I explained.

"That's cool, man. I know how those concerts go, right on. Is that girl cute? You got a little crush on her dude?" she asked, chuckling as she tried to embarrass me in front of Drew.

"Ah stop," I chuckled, "we're gonna go hangout upstairs and probably sleep. Our friends will be here tomorrow, then we can all go to the beach."

"Awesome, see you dudes tomorrow," she said and walked back to the couch.

I woke up that morning realizing how nice it is to have a bed. After all, I had been sleeping on a surfboard in the van for the past week. The sun was just beginning to rise over the horizon to the faint sound of one of my aunt's neighbors playing guitar. I woke up and I grabbed my surfboard and headed down to the beach. My favorite part of Mexico was definitely the fact I didn't need a wetsuit. Without a wetsuit, getting out in the morning was less of an ordeal.

I got to the beach and laid down my board before plopping down on my ass. I started strumming my guitar, trying different combinations of the few chords I knew. I'm sure it sounded like ass, but nobody was up, but eventually I stopped feeling the music and instead started feeling the gentle rumble of the crashing, easy going waves. Only 4 feet tall but with a good deal of power and the rides looked like they'd last forever. I smoked the 3 joints I brought down with me to properly blastoff before paddling out.

My lungs burned, but it was a good burn, the kind that comes through heavy exercise. I got to the peak on my 9 foot longboard. Within a minute a solid wave started to form, I paddled and paddled, ending with one big double stroke before popping up to drop in. I banked right as soon as I could and charged down the face. It was a longboard, but I was surfing it like a shortboard, throwing everything I had into making a somewhat sharp turn before slowing down, relaxing, and dancing up to the top. Now the tune of the this wave, the song of the ocean, had mellowed out. No longer was I just trying to go as hard as possible, I was sitting back, and relaxing. When I got down past the middle of the board, I did it literally. I just sat down on the board and rode the wave into the shore before tumbling onto the ground. Below me the warm Mexican water, above me a blue sky with the colors of the sun bleeding into it. Directly in front was the rising sun. It was amazingly peaceful, again I was in that blissful state so often felt during this road trip.

10 minutes had passed, just laying there, the tide was beginning to shift so I packed up and headed back to get my breakfast. I assumed nobody was up yet so I was going to spear a fish and grab eggs from the store, make like a seafood breakfast fry.

Diving was difficult at first, but as I swam out, the physical effects of the weed slowly wore off and the cerebral lingered. There was something about this place that made it easy to keep in that balanced state of mind. I floated there, breathing calmly and launching myself into a meditative state that was in sync with the peaceful rock reef I was gazing at below. Just before I dove, I took 3 large breaths to pump my blood with the oxygen it needed. As I went deeper into the crystal, blue water, the temperature began to drop a bit, not much, but enough the water was cool. It was like taking a walk on a warm spring day with a cool breeze wrapping around my body.

With an unsuccessful first dive, I went back up for air and felt the warm summer sun, now about an eighth of the way on its rise. I felt recharged after a couple minutes, ready for another dive so down I went. Something felt a bit off, like I should just go in and buy fish at the store, but I went anyway. At around fifty five feet down, I saw a bigass amberjack, bigger than any I'd seen before. I got as close as I could to it before firing a perfectly place shot. It didn't fight much given that its spinal chord had been severed, and I instantly began swimming up to the surface. My lungs burned from the carbon dioxide trapped inside and screamed to be filled with oxygen. Exhaling felt like a huge relief, and the following breath was welcomed like an old friend.

Right as I brained the fish, I saw it. About 55 feet out I saw it, a fin accompanied by a large black body. I strung my catch and swam faster than I ever swam. I tried not to look back, but I did and was overcome with a panic previously unbeknownst to me. I had caught the attention of a bull shark, and a big one at that.

I kept swimming and just as it got to me I was to shallow for it to follow, but It took a bite out of my fin. It's razor sharp teeth went straight through the carbon fiber, but I was still able to emerge from the water unscathed. I ran onto the now warm sand and threw myself on it, more grateful than I ever have been to be on land. I just survived a shark attack and I kept my catch, an achievement not many could boast. It would've been much smarter to leave my catch behind so the shark would have lost interest in me, but damn, it was one hell of a fish. I cleaned the fish about a half mile down the beach, hopefully bringing the shark over there and away from the reef near my surf spot. Afterwards, I packed up, bringing all my stuff up and leaving it in my car. All that I brought in was the fish and the battle-scarred fin.

After filleting the fish and starting to cook it, my aunt walked downstairs. First, she saw was me cooking, and then, she saw the thing that made her shout, "Kevin! Did a shark bite your fin?!?"

"Just the tip, it's good. I think Drew has a spare pair," I cooly responded.

"You could've died!"

"But I didn't."

"Well, smells like some damn good fish, I wouldn't have let go of it either," she said with a smile and started making coffee.

"What's all that noise? You asswipes woke me up... wait... shit that's the second time this has happened dumbass! Learn to let go of a fish because I only have one spare pair of fins left!" Drew said, groggy and pissed, but amused nonetheless.

"I don't think even you would've let go of this amberjack, and I've seen you drop fish because of something as small as a sandbar shark!" I responded.

"Amberjack? Nice, well I'm gonna go sleep on the couch, I'm fuckin' dead man," Drew said.

My aunt stopped doing what she was doing and smacked him on the back of the head. That poor kid, she was gonna do to him what she did to me: turn him into a morning person.

Ever since I was little she's forced me to get up early and be productive (she used to live down the street from Skip). So much so that if I sleep past nine, I still feel as though I wasted my entire day, but it's caused me to actually do something with my time, ultimately making me actually enjoy life. On the other hand, learning to be a productive human was not fun, and Drew was about to get a crash course in what my aunt spent years doing to me during our short stay in Baja.

"Well, if I'm supposed to be awake what do I do? If there's nothing to do I should just sleep!" Drew said, interrupting my aunt's rant that I'd zoned out on while cooking, which was near done by now.

"Nothing to do? There's always something to do! If there's any time you've seen anybody do anything and thought 'whoa that's cool, that'd be kinda cool to do', then just do it. What've you thought that's cool, ya know other than being a bum?" my Aunt responded.

"I dunno, I always thought it'd be cool to play the drums. I saw an old video of that dude in Rush wailing on some drums and thought that was pretty wicked," Drew answered.

"Then learn the drums!"

"There's no drums here!"

"Not a big set, but we have drums!"

"Where?"

"Anything is a drum if you try hard enough."

"That's the biggest load of BS I've heard in my whole damn life!"

"You sure about that? I don't know about you,

but I've seen some street performers with a couple buckets make a sound unlike any I've ever heard. We do have drums, try these bongos. Just do whatever and have fun with it. That's what music is all about, anyway, if music is even about anything," my aunt finished saying as she handed him an old, weathered set of bongos.

Drew looked at them with a funky look on his face, inspecting them at all angles, tapping a bit here and there, like a curious little kitten. He hit the hembra (the larger of the drums), then hit it again and again before starting a little beat. Although my back was turned, I quickly could tell when he began incorporating the macho into what he was playing, and then the beat really picked up. My aunt grabbed her guitar and started playing with him, making a random jam song, and it was just the best song I'd heard on any morning. There truly was nothing like listening to two people jam, cooking fresh caught fish, and being able to look out at the ocean.

The food was amazing, we all sat down and chowed down. Even my petite aunt, got a large second serving. Just as we were finishing breakfast up, we heard a knock at the door. I shot up out of my seat, plate still at the table, and ran to the door. By the time my hand wrapped around the handle I was panting and red faced. I opened the door to Feather and Lauralyn and gave them huge hugs.

"Come on in guys! There should still be some breakfast left!" I said, excited as hell.

"Good to see you too man! We went to the wrong place 3 times but still managed to get here quick. I love it down here already!" Feather responded.

"Wait til you get out on the water! You'll

really love it then, but we have to postpone that for a day," I said. Just then we walked into the house and darted to the kitchen and grabbed the scarred fin.

"Oh my god Kevin! You could've died! I'm so glad you're okay!" Laura shouted as she ran over and hugged me.

"Chill out Laura, he's alive still, sadly," Feather said and we both laughed, "now let's eat what he should've died to get!"

That day we went a bit further south to find some good, non-sharky surf, but on our way down I pointed out we were only an hour from Cabo. So, now with Feather driving my van, we headed down to Cabo. Watching Feather drive was an experience in it's own. Once the sound system blew out from him blasting The Doors way too loud, he proceeded in singing every song that came into his head, and he wasn't bad at it either! In fact, he was good, real good. That's when I had an idea, better than the one I'd thought the day before. I'd sit on it for now, but so far, I saw each of us had some kind of musical talent. If Laura could play bass, the four of us could start a band.

The spot we pulled over at took priority over any kind of day dreaming. The waves were big and it looked like it was time to breakout the shortboard. They were heavy waves, but every time I lasted through the drop, I got an awesome barrel ride before being spitted out the front of the barrel at a million miles an hour with a wall of white water at my back. This was by far the biggest I ever surfed, the waves were between ten and fifteen feet in height, and I felt every inch of the size as the sheer power of the wave launched me down the line. On the longboard I felt all the serenity and calmness the ocean had to offer, and then I felt the extreme power, speed, and adrenaline provided by the waves. The best part? Whether it's one foot waves and whitewash, or ten, fifteen, even twenty foot leviathans, a day surfing was a day surfing and it was fun no matter what. Just like a day living is a day living, so might as well make it fun no matter what. That's what we all were doing too, just doing what it took to have fun and enjoy life.

I looked to the beach and saw it was empty, nobody was filming us here. This wasn't some huge contest. We were all surfing our hearts out even though nobody was there because that's what it was all about. Even Laura was in the water, body surfing the white wash since she was a new surfer and would probably die surfing this. Although fun, we paddled in. Feather and Laura had brought a bunch of junk food down with them so we went to the van, chowed down, smoked a bit, munched some more, and then I pulled out my guitar. Drew already was pounding out a beat on the drum and I joined in. We were going back and forth making a beautiful rhythm. The beach didn't sound like waves crashing or seagulls, it sounded like the music you make when it takes over and possesses your very being. I realized in that moment, and every moment since I'd left New York, I was the beach. It had raised me and I never left it, nor did I have any desire to do so.

After a short lived second wind, Laura was the first to go in, and Drew quickly followed suit. Then, it was only Feather and I remaining on the water. In the distance I heard the sound of Drew banging on bongos accompanied by what sounded like a bass guitar. Feather turned to look at me and we both knew where this was going.

"So, Kevin, how's it going with the guitar?" Feather asked.

"I've learned much, much quicker than I thought I would."

"What do you say we go in and join them for a little jam session?"

"I think that's a grand fuckin' idea, man."

GOOD VIBRATIONS

An hour later we were sitting in the van in Cabo jamming out. Laura's bass turned out to be a janky little thing she made from a plank and an empty cigar box, but that didn't take away the fact it still sounded pretty good. First, Drew would lay down a beat, and then Laura would join him with a bass line. After those two started, Feather and I would look at each other and simultaneously join in with guitar and vocals. Half of what Feather said was complete gibberish, if you actually thought about the lyrics, but the words he sang sounded amazing when they combined with the sound of the instruments vibrating through the air. We kept the routine going for a good couple hours more, watching the sunset and whatnot.

"We really need a name for this thing," Feather said, talking about the Westfalia.

"We could paint it too!" I responded.

"Well what the hell do we call it, it's a brokedown old van," Drew said.

"I say we name it after what we do with it. So far we've been doing things that could get us in a bunch of trouble in it," I said.

"You guys have traveled a bunch with it to and I think we're gonna travel a lot more in it. I say we call it the Travelin' Trouble Machine, or TTM for short," Laura said.

"I like it! I'll drive to the store and I can grab

some paint tomorrow morning, but for now, we have some business to attend to. It's summer and we're in Cabo, let's fuckin' party!" Feather exclaimed as he climbed down and swung back into the driver seat through the window.

The four of us were at a bar within an hour and people are age began to flood in after an additional 30 minutes. Groups of girls flocked to Drew, Feather, and I, given that we fit the look every girl was looking for. Three surfers with tan skin, ratty hair (except Drew, he kept it clean, Feather let his go wild over the course of his road trip), and scruffy, sun-kissed faces. Although, I could've cared less about everybody around us, I just went over to a corner in the club with two Tecates and sat down with Laura, but I realized that although she was attractive as all hell, I couldn't see her beyond a simple friend. We finished them quickly before Drew sat down and Feather followed with a shot for everybody. I downed it, the bitter tequila burned and warmed my insides as I felt it hit my stomach. I knew it was going to be quite the night. It had only been a short while, I was already buzzing, and the small club was starting to fill up pretty fast. Music started thumping, and it was the kind with the heavy bass you can feel deep in the pit of your stomach that added a whole other sense to the musical experience. It was the kind that connected to your soul not necessarily through lyrics, but through the physical feeling of the music itself.

Laura got up and came back with a plate of more shots and two margaritas, "Some guys straight up just bought me these two margaritas in the five minutes I was waiting for more tequila!" And that's when I realized, I didn't feel a bit jealous, when a week ago, I would've been turned green.

We all finished our drinks and I stood up. Transformed by the poison running through my blood, I was more outgoing, less laid back and ready for a real party. I grabbed Laura by the hand and we went to the dance floor and danced for an hour before the first band began setting up. They were going to have live music and I saw this as a perfect opportunity, as there was no security. Halfway into the set I learned that the band to follow this one up wasn't going to play that night, so I hatched a little plan and brought Laura with me back over to Drew and Feather.

"Laura, Feather, either of you have some LSD left?" I asked.

"Ya, my cousin gave us a bunch more, he knows a guy who makes it, why?" Feather asked.

"How much more?"

"He gave it to us in a liquid vial, we have probably around 200 trips worth of LSD, why Kevin?"

"Get a pitcher of lemonade, I have an idea," I said.

"Well what the hell is your idea already," Drew said, laughing but somewhat frustrated at my beating around the bush.

"Well what if we just went up there and jammed and we could give out glasses of lemonade with LSD in it for five bucks. We can make some money and we get to play!" I answered.

"Why are we giving them acid though?" Laura asked.

"So they're on the same level as us, obviously we're going to enjoy some to ourselves! Plus, I don't think we're quite the musicians we wish we were yet,

37

it'll help them think we're a lot better than we are," I answered.

I went up to the manager of the bar telling him that we heard they needed somebody else to play, I told him we'd do it and all we wanted was a couple free drinks.   He was more than happy to oblige and informed me that this band would be done in a half hour and we could set up when they're done. I went outside with a pitcher of margarita that we got virgin so we could add our special ingredient. We got out our instruments, and put them down behind the stage before pouring ourselves a couple cups of our drinks. I looked at the guitar Bob gave me and thought, *the first time I actually use this with an amp, and I'm playing in front of 50 people! I can barely play! Maybe Lucy can give me a hand.*

While the first band was finishing up I was going through their guitarist's bag looking at chord charts and trying to play them until it sounded right. I felt really comfortable and I was ready to just play what I felt, what this place made feel, how being on the water made me feel. I told the other band they could have a free cup of lemonade each if they let us use some of their equipment and they agreed right away. Feather then took the microphone and announced: "I'm Feather, this is Laura, the one with the bongos is Drew, and that one is Kevin, and he is really starting to trip his goddamn balls off. The first time we played together was this morning and we just took some acid so this is going to be interesting. Come on up and get a cup for five bucks, you'll really regret it if you don't, you don't wanna hear us sober."

Drew played first since he was hit first.   I looked over at him and he was playing those bongos like it was all he was supposed to do in life. It had only been two minutes, but he was jamming so hard that little beads of cool sweat were already rolling down his forehead. Laura joined in next dropping a smooth bass line, and I shortly followed her, throwing in my guitar.

The nervousness and anxiety began to fade as soon as I started playing the guitar, and it completely vanished in the moment I began to come up, which was simultaneous with Feather adding his vocals. At first, he was just spouting random nonsense to the sound of music, and then he started to recite what had to be poetry, but I had no idea who wrote it (maybe the man himself did). The pitcher was empty and Feather got down to refill it when somebody random handed him a harmonica, and I could tell his eyes lit up in that instant.

Feather pulled the vial out of his pocket and emptied the three quarters left of it into the pitcher, swirling it around a bit, before taking three big gulps, putting the harmonica to his lips, and playing on his way to the stage. All the while people followed behind him in this kind of this conga line of vacationers who were starting to trip out to our music. Feather climbed back to the stage and this winding line of people continued, each one wanting to get their share of the drink after seeing how much fun we all were having.

"Hello, it's your captain, Feather, speaking once more my friends. Feel free to video tape us and trip your FUCKing balls off. Thank you very much ladies and gentlemen. Now please, fasten your seat belts and prepare for blast off," Feather announced, we all stopped playing to listen to him "I hope you all enjoyed our warm up as much as we did. As we draw closer to our peaks we get closer to our show, we're...

um... the Waterboys! No, not the waterboys, none of us are Adam Sandler. We're... uh... the Blue Boys! Ah shit no, Laura doesn't have a dick, um... we're Euphoria! No... um... we're Euphoric Blue!" Feather said, the effects of the drug obviously had taken a heavy hold.

As soon as he said the name a little ring went off in my head, I started to play, wildly and without a clear direction. I just played how I felt, something that words and even music couldn't describe. It took about ten minutes for the next instrument to join in, Drew's bongos, as we were all heavily tripping. I saw some pyramids in the distance and I swear I felt some warm desert breeze wash over my whole body as I was wrapped, wrapped up in this swirling cocoon of ever changing colors. No longer did I see the crowd, it was just me and my guitar in our own little sheltered place. I could play whatever the hell I wanted, I could play the journey I was going on.

My playing picked up and up, getting softer and lighter as I did. Slowly the music began to be drowned out by a loud ringing, the source seemed to be inside my head, right in the direct center. Then I looked down, I was still there, playing my guitar, my whole body changing color to the song. *Holy fucking spaghetti monster, I'm floating, floating above my goddamn body... chillout... hey this sounds kinda good... can I fly-WHOA...Whoa... I just fucking flew out of my own body and now I'm flying. Holy shit I need to close my eyes-*

CRASH! And I was thrown out of this whole dimension, there's no way to explain it. I still heard the music we were playing as the tunnel I flew through pulsed and wavered before I was spit back out and thrown into my body. Faces shot by me in this tunnel that I'd not yet seen, I saw a grave accompanied by an empty chair. A beautiful colored bird flew overhead as it picked me up in its talons, carrying me back to the now, the present, where I was dropped back in front of my body. I stared directly into my own eyes as I sat there and played, my head turned, I smiled, and I walked back in.

The club was empty, everybody had left hours ago but none of has had stopped playing. The moon had nearly completed its journey across the sky, I think Apollo had about two hours before his 12 hour break. Six and a half hours had passed, yet it felt like 10 minutes... did it? I wasn't sure at this point, I still felt some effects of the drug, so now was not the time to think, or else I'd be stuck in a thought loop. My ears still had a very distant ringing and I no longer had the desire to smoke in the morning. I realized that I was abusing the drug and ran the risk of doing the same with LSD if I wasn't able to respect the substance. It was time to go sober for a while, but what it had just showed me was life changing. No longer did I fear death, I feared that I wouldn't truly live.

RISE

We got back to my aunt's house with faces showing how tired we were and passed out wherever there was room. Laura slept on the floor below the couch I was snoozing on, Drew and Feather were strung out near each other on a mattress of pillows. By the time the sun was beginning its ascent, my aunt woke us up and told us to "get off our lazy asses and do something!" Apparently laying around and trying to catch up on sleep wasn't something enough, so I went into her garage and grabbed all the paint I could find.

There were all sorts of crazy colors, most were bright and vibrant. I grabbed some brushes, but there were also quite a few cans of spray paint. The whole crew was waiting outside by the van, including my aunt, they all knew what I wanted to do when I went to find the paint.

INNN about an hour or so, the van had transformed from your boring, old, stock Westfalia, to a kickass, colorful mess. This thing was definitely going to be turning heads wherever we went, and to top it all off, I spray painted a big "TTM" on the side.

"Where even were you guys last night?" Ann asked.

"We went to a club in Cabo, and, well, we got a bit carried away. We actually ended up jamming on stage since they needed a band to play," I answered.

"You're crazy! Well if you want any equipment to play more, the dude down the street has a bunch of stuff. Him and a couple other guys used to have a little band," my aunt explained.

"Ah shit! Let's go Kevin! I think we've got to get back stateside. Everybody pile in! We're getting that gear and heading north! Thanks Miss Kevin's Aunt!" Feather said as he took the van keys out of my hand.

"Come back down again sometime!" she chimed.

It didn't take long before we were back in San Diego, or at least it didn't seem to take too long. Laura and I slept most of the way after leaving Pescadero while Drew and Feather took turns driving, until Feather made a pitstop to buy an unhealthy amount of energy drinks. After that, we all had to take turns sitting shotgun to keep Feather company as he rambled and ranted. Most of the time I'd fall asleep during one of his rants and I'd wake up an hour later to him being on a completely different topic. This guy just went on and on, whatever went on inside of his head must be insane, or maybe he just said what he thought out loud...

"Feather, do you just say everything you think?" I asked, causing him to take a momentary pause (something he only did when he slept, although, Feather was a bit of a sleep-talker).

"Most of it. If it's worth thinking, it's sure as hell worth saying. I think if everybody just said what they thought instead of what somebody else thought we'd all get along much better," Feather explained.

"What about the people who think stupid

things? They just end up saying stupid things, what do they do?" Laura chimed in.

"Well, it seems like they just run for president. PERSONALLY I think it's a good thing that they do, that way other stupid people will flock to them, and that way we can put them all in their little corner of idiocracy," Feather responded.

"But what if the majority of people are stupid?" Drew questioned.

"Well then the stupid people get what they want, then we're probably fucked, but we could always just come down here," Feather answered.

"Feather, you're the last person I'd see just not doing anything about a cruddy politician doing a cruddy job and turning the whole country into a goddamn pile of... well crud!" I said, grinning, my statement met by some giggles from the backseat.

"Well why would I try and fix somebody else's crud pile when I can keep my pile of... um... not crud?" Feather said. Although it was one of the most "high guy" responses I've heard, it made me think, but just as my head began hurting from thinking exponentially harder than I normally do, the car lurched forward. Feather had the look in his eyes of a madman, well more so than normal, and he was gassing the car on the freeway, heeding nobody. Weaving between lanes and other cars with a huge grin on his face. He was making this old piece of junk go faster than I ever thought it could... oh... no... there's traffic, and a lot of it.

From my point of view we were zipping along, when really we were really only going about 40 miles an hour, but that was much faster than anybody should go in the traffic we were in. Each maneuver that Feather made came down to the centimeter, if he was off by even just one of those tiny little metric units, we would've had quite the accident on our hands.

"FEATHER WHAT THE HELL ARE YOU DOING, YOU'RE GOING TO CRASH THIS VAN," Laura shouted from the back.

"I know exactly what I'm doing thank you very much, now calm down. Close your eyes if it helps, take a nap, I don't care, just don't do that or I will crash!" Feather responded, almost pissed off (something he never was).

It was the craziest 45 minutes of driving I'd ever experienced, but in Feather's defense he did know what he was doing and the TTM wasn't in a single accident- well not that day at least. Soon we were in LA, getting gas and I knew we were going to be holed up here for a little while. Feather went into a store and came out with an intercom system and what looked like small handrails. I moved to go help him, but Laura stopped me and explained that he was in his zone, and when he's in his zone he needs to just be in it and do what he needs to do.

What he ended up needing to do was setting up the speaker equipment on the roof of the Vanagon, which he outfitted with rails that came up to hip level. He hooked up the intercom system to the sound system on top and we all knew what he wanted to do. Nobody but Ethan Feather was crazy enough to think of driving around a mobile stage through LA with a bunch of dirty surfers who barely knew how to play their respective instruments, all the while sitting atop a van with TTM, random psychedelic art, and a few hidden penises spray painted on the side.

Oh man oh man, here we go. Why are we even

45

doing this? How in the hell does Feather think of these things, is this even legal? Ah well, Feather hasn't been wrong, I thought to myself.

The mix of adrenaline, excitement, nervousness, and something I couldn't explain were swirling around inside my body, feeble in comparison the the intense emotions I felt. At first, people were extremely confused, and they were just blankly staring in an attempt to comprehend what was going on in front of them. People were trying to figure out what was going on, and what the hell was rolling through downtown LA, but it was until people realized that it was people going through LA. Some of these aforementioned people realized they could be like us and a couple of them started following us and Feather slowed down. Pretty soon it grew from five, to ten, to about forty five people until we heard the sound of a police siren, to which Feather promptly replied "fuck off brah! We're trying to have a parade here!" and kept on going. That little line made around another thirty people join in on our impromptu and unsanctioned parade, but it didn't matter to them, they were just trying to have a good time.

"Kevin! I need you to throw drugs at these people!" Feather yelled from the window.

"You want me to throw drugs at the people following us in a van through downtown LA while we have cops popping up out of nowhere?" I replied in disbelief, not even Feather was this crazy... was he?

"Yes, that's exactly what I want you to do, my fellow!" yes in fact, Feather was that crazy.

Shit, Feather was even crazier as it takes a certain kind of insane individual to start chanting, "we're giving people psychedelics! We're giving people psychedelics!   We're giving people psychedelics! Now they're gonna have a good time and a good trip, probably question your authority a bit too! Ha ha hahaha ha!" while I threw a couple bags of shrooms and blotters of LSD in clear wrap off the back of our very colorful bus (obviously taking some myself and giving them to my bandmates, I didn't give any to Feather as I assume at that point he was already well ahead of us in that department, and driving).

Our following grew to about a hundred people and Feather had stopped passing up our magic lil' teachers, but that's when a smell of a certain burning plant reached my nose that was all too familiar at this point. We'd ran out before crossing the border, but the crowd obviously was well supplied, and pretty soon, we had around 200 people high, tripping, or all of the above marching around to our slightly above average music being played atop a sketchy looking van.

Feather led our soon to be students to a small park where he promptly drove up onto the sidewalk and into the middle of the park. We stopped the music for a second while he got out more speakers and a real microphone.   Drew looked at Feather and nodded, Feather took out some maracas (where he got them, to this day I have no idea whatsoever), and Drew began playing a beat that was very familiar to all of us and Feather chimed in.   Lauralyn added the baseline and Feather started singing Sympathy for the Devil. There were cops who'd followed us to the park and were starting to walk up to our set, but more and more people started filling in recognizing the song. The pigs weren't having it.   To them we were breaking laws; traffic laws, federal drug laws, all sorts of rules and laws put in place to keep people complacent, but the officers were having a bit of trouble getting to us due to the group of around 350 people making a barrier around our little van, sharing this jam session with us, thoroughly enjoying themselves, everybody on the drug of their choice: pot, shrooms, LSD, cocaine, or just life, and enjoying this spontaneous little concert.

I was so absorbed in what was going on around me that I barely realized I was supposed to do the last solo of the song, I'd played it multiple times in the car and nailed it every time, but never before was my guitar a fuzzy three-headed snake with frets and strings made of long taquitos and tiny tacos. It didn't matter though, I just played my heart out when I heard Feather say, "Hey man, I get you're doing your job and all, but we're not hurting anybody, give us tickets if you need after our show, but just let us play! Nobody's getting hurt, we're just playin some music, come and enjoy officers!"

The boys in blue were visibly taken aback, but, one by one, the six or seven officers came and joined in the growing crowd in this little park. For his next trick, Feather started singing Hound Dog, and I have no idea how, but we all managed to play the golden oldie. It sounded great, we didn't even have a real drum set! (Drew had picked up a snare drum at a secondhand music store in San Diego, but his drum set consisted of a single snare, bongos, and two buckets) The crowd kept building and building, and we just started playing our own songs with Feather just making lyrics up on the spot when he'd feel them come on, and when he'd lose it I'd solo, and when I'd lose it Drew would solo, and so on and so forth.

We stopped for a minute, gathered ourselves and I was no longer absorbed in playing my outlandish, ever changing instrument. It was back to the guitar I knew, but the crowd had grown, it was massive, tens of thousands of people, and we weren't even in the park anymore! Behind me was a slightly aged Drew (wasn't looking too hot, though) with a real drum set. Laura was to my right with a beautiful bass and hair down past her waist, but Feather was nowhere to be seen. I was confused as to what I was looking at, a stage I didn't recognize, a shitload of people, and bandmates who were a bit older than when I saw them a couple seconds ago. To top it all off, it looked like we were in front of some sort of protest.

"Kevin, play your song, are you with us buddy? You know the one, you played it nonstop when you were awake. Come on back Kevin, come onnnn," I heard Feather say to me, disoriented and not quite back yet, although I was able to distinguish that I in fact was not headlining a protest.

I wasn't sure what Feather was talking about, but I started with the intro to Johnny B Goode before following it up with the rest of the song. Feather sang and danced like the maniac he was and I went into a solo like none I'd ever played before. For some reason Lucy took my hand and brought me to the future, I don't know why, but whatever the reason, it looked like I was in for an interesting ride.

MONEY

Feather drove the Travelin' Trouble Machine up to San Francisco and we decided to settle down for a while. After getting recognized all over the place as "those dudes who played music on top of a van" or "those hippies who had a random concert in a park", we realized that we needed to work on getting some real equipment. First order of business was getting Drew a real drumset and then we needed to hook Laura up with a kickass bass. We definitely get some better amps and maybe get a storage unit and some recording equipment to get a demo out, but there was one problem.

"Money. We have fucking none of it," Drew said, staring at a nice set with a longing look on his face.

"Fuck money man, it's the root of greed, and greed, greed is the root of fucking all evil," Feather said.

"Ya, but things like food, gas, and equipment cost money, Ethan. We're not in Mexico anymore, it's not like we can just spearfish and surf all day forever," Laura retorted.

"Well, we could," Feather replied.

"We'd also be bums! Ethan, do you realize the opportunity we have, we're internet famous, and that could turn to real fame! We have a chance to do something big," Laura said.

"Fame means jack shit! I don't wanna be

famous, I wanna be happy! Everybody famous who says something worth saying ends up dead or selling their soul! I wanna just do what I like," Feather said.

"Ethan, you're good at what you like. You don't have to do it for the money or the fame, but do it to spread all these great ideas you have! Think about all the people who recognized us from watching videos of us playing in a park, now imagine if we actually put ourselves to work, actually go out and make our own music. You can put whatever message you want in every song you write and people will listen to that song, and they're going to hear that message. You can tell people all these things you always talk to me about, wage slavery, some corporate elite ruling us, or whatever other hippie shit you wanna sing about, but thousands of other people are going to hear it, maybe even millions, Feather, you can be the change you're always talking about. But, I swear, if we stop right now and you decide to go be a beach bum and I ever hear you bitch about something that you could've changed through music, so help me God, I'm going to slap you until there's no cheek left to slap!"

"Um... well... I guess we're getting jobs then!" Feather said and grabbed a newspaper to look through the job ads.

About six months had passed and we were all (but Feather) working miserable jobs for miserable wages, but we were getting done what we needed to get done. The four of us lived in this miserable studio apartment with no real furniture, just a small stage we made from soap boxes, a bunch of beanbag chairs, and four mattresses on the ground. We had enough saved up to get Drew a solid drum set, Laura a good bass, sound equipment, and I got myself a little ukulele, one of the greatest investments I've ever made. See with with a uke, you can play anywhere, any time, and you can bring it with you wherever you go and just play to your heart's desire. Lighter and cheaper than a guitar, it's the ultimate little travel instrument, and, over those six months, I got much better at guitar, but also learned to wail on the uke, which I think is much more important since that was purely for personal enjoyment, and that's by far the most important thing in life. I mean honestly, most people say life is too short to be miserable, but a wiseman once said life's way too long to be miserable! Imagine that, 80 plus years of everything just doing nothing other than completely sucking ass. That'd just be all kinds of awful! I digress, I got a bit sidetracked there, so enough about me and more about Feather, who's the whole reason you're reading this.

So Feather, he's spent those first few months simply trying to get hired, and eventually gave up and just started singing on street corners. This left him with countless hours of freetime (and barely enough money to buy lunch each day). So, with these countless hours of freetime he wrote countless lyrics. At first, they were barely mediocre, but at the end of this six month period, Feather was writing some of the most amazing lyrics I'd seen in my years on this planet. There were a couple about girls, love, and bangin', but for the most part, he was telling stories, stories of his life through the lyrics he wrote, stories he made up, and making comments on today's world. The recent election of President Trump and the complete screwing over of other political candidates earlier on in the race were central to some of his songs, and the lazy bums running our country who won't make any laws other than ones that raise their salary earned themselves their own song as well. One of my personal favorite songs he wrote at this time was about the fall of Rome, Feather found a way to recap the events in an interesting way, but when you really look into it, it's talking about the fall of our country. Each and every parallel was outlined between Rome's fall to what's going on now: crumbling infrastructure, dirty water, attacks from small military groups, and people in power who definitely shouldn't have it. "Complete and utter psychos" if you will.

But, for the rest of us, it wasn't just work, otherwise we'd all be too miserable. Every Sunday we got together and surfed from Carmel point all the way back up to Ocean Beach, starting around six in the morning and ending at about seven in the evening. Afterwards we'd do what we do best and throw a party in our studio apartment that wasn't so miserable on those Sunday nights. At first, people would show up at around 12 in the afternoon and smoke some pot while we'd go and play our music while equally high. Then, each week, more and more people started coming since their friend told them about some "kickass hippie band who just let's us smoke at their place while they play!", and it got to the point where every Sunday we'd have about 200 people in our apartment. So many more wanted to come, and we had to have Feather do a sign-up sheet while he sang on the streets, and if you weren't on the list, you couldn't get in, but to avoid having the same faces all the time, unless you were apart of those first twelve, you could only get on that list if you weren't at the party in the past two weeks.

It was after that six month period that things

really started to get insane. Since we had so many people coming we started charging ten bucks at the door, pulling us in a cool eight thousand a month. That eight thousand was enough to cover rent and start our own indoor garden (we grew some vegetables in addition to our cannabis and psychedelic plants and fungi). As the crowd diversified, the types of substances used began to follow suit. Our one rule was no needles, they were a pain to clean up and we didn't really want people chasing any dragons through our apartment, that can create quite the mess with all the fire and all. What was going on in our place began to look like the Acid Tests taking place in the same city 50 years ago, so we decided to take advantage of this and teach the people somethin'.

A punch bowl of Lucy and a pizza with some shroomies, we had people trippin' their goddamn nuts off. We'd party through the entire night and each time we'd finish, Feather would stand by the door, ask people their name, write it down, ask what they learned, and write that down. If they didn't learn anything he'd turn them back and tell them to sit down until they found something new about themselves or the world. If they said something they've already said (that guy Feather has quite the memory), then he'd send them right back to the end of the line.

Another six months passed, and we had about 500 people we were rotating in and out of our apartment every Sunday night, and at the same time we were dedicating our entire beings to making music. As we tripped more, we began learning more, but myself, Feather, and Laura stopped tripping each time because we didn't need to. We only tripped when we knew there was something we'd learn, when we felt that we truly had to. But Drew, he kept at it. In fact, his dosages began to skyrocket, and at this time he also began experimenting with cocaine. "Only on special occasions," he said, but I knew there weren't three different special occasions a week. It wasn't my place to intervene, though. At the time I just thought I'd let it work itself out and he'd stop doing blow, but that's not how it works.

Feather began to take what he learned from the next plane up, and he started incorporating it in the songs he was writing. The next three songs he wrote had changed tone from comments on today's society to what can only be compared to the preaching of a psychonaut, or an explorer of the human mind. Feather was fascinated to how things worked. He spent less and less time actually writing songs as he did gathering material to write about. Drew, Laura, and I would leave to surf or spearfish or crab, and we'd leave Feather meditating, and then come back around seven hours later and he'd be in the same spot, unmoved. Eventually I asked him, "Feather, the hell are you trying to get out of all this meditating. I mean shit, the only time you do anything else is when you wanna write or on our Pizza Parties!"

"That's the point, I don't know what I'm trying to get out of it. I'm trying to find an answer to a question that I don't know how to ask. Hell, I don't even have an idea of why I want to ask the question!" Feather replied.

"Then why spend so much time trying to find the question to ask? It sounds kind of like the question is what is the question, but if you're just trying to figure out the question to be asked, what's the point? I mean, why not just, do your thing and chill?"

"I've gotta find the answer! There has to be a reason for all the bullshit going on. I mean we've got it easy, we have no worries, we're not apart of what they're apart of, the machine, why do people allow it to control their lives? Why does it exist in the first place? Why don't people just fucking leave it? I mean everybody who comes here deals with unnecessary stress and bullshit six days of the week and they all come to realize it doesn't matter, but they don't leave! Why the hell not?"

"I think those are a few different answers, man. Look, Ethan, you're not finding that answer if you try and find it. It'll show itself to you, show itself to all of us, when we can't look anymore because we realize we don't need to, it doesn't matter. Whether you have the answer or not, life will go on and the world will keep spinning until it doesn't."

"But Kevin, you gotta understand that I haven't had a normal life. I haven't ever been involved with society or anything. Lauralyn was my only friend when I stopped hangin with the fuckers I used to skate with. That mattress on the floor over there is the closest thing to a real bed I've slept in for 4 years. There has to be a reason for all the suffering everybody goes through, that I've gone through."

"Shit happens, and it's either bad or good, but whatever what happens is bad or good is your choice. Some things happen that are just too hard to have a positive outlook on, but you're hanging onto the bad shit that's happened, and that's why you're suffering. That's why everybody suffers. Everybody suffers, but it's your choice to continue to suffer, or to end that suffering at the moment and be happy until the next moment of suffering comes and the cycle starts over again."

"Fuck man... but there has to be a reason why everybody is suffering more than they should. What's the difference between me and the businessmen who walk by when I'm performing at BART?"

"Well, what's the difference between them and you?"

"They've got money for one thing, they also-"

"Stop right there Feather. That's the difference. They have money and it's because they work 9-5 everyday in some big office that's cramped, artificial, and inside. Not only are these people wasting their lives away, but they know they're doing so, but it's in the pursuit of some piece of paper which is overall worthless without somebody telling us it's worth something. These individuals then go and try to get more to validate themselves so they can have a better car than their neighbor or some other meaningless piece of shit some commercial told them to go buy."

"Fuck Kevin, sometimes I think you should be writing these songs, man."

"Good one Feather, that's all you, I'm just here to play guitar. We haven't all really played together in a while."

"Are you thinking what I'm thinking?"

"I really hope so."

Feather in fact was thinking what I was thinking, but even better. Within two hours we were at the Jerry Garcia Amphitheater (without anybody's permission to do so but our own, but I think Jerry would've been cool with it), and we'd called all 500 of our "students", for lack of a better word. We got our gear set up and familiar faces started filling the seats. Drew set up his drumset but was nowhere to be found. All of us went into panic mode as more and more people started filling in, the crowd was close to double the size it was 20 minutes beforehand and we had no drummer.

"Right here... I'm good," Drew said, his words slurring.

"God dammit are you drunk?" Laura asked.

"Just a bit... I'm good. If I get too tired I've got a pick me up," Drew answered.

"Alright, we're all good then, everybody, let's get goin, Kevin, you start us off," Feather said and sighted.

"Alright guys tonight, tonight I'm feeling high energy and real fun. We'll start out with some Stones, move on to Zeppelin, and then I want you Feather, I want you to finish off the last three songs with something you've been writing. I know we haven't really played any of them, but hell, we've done way crazier shit than winging instrumentals to prewritten lyrics. This is bigger than anything we've done, it's time to show people Euphoric Blue," I said in an attempt to motivate my two nervous bandmates, but Feather was already in his zone.

We walked out to around 1500 people, and were met with applause from those who frequent our apartment. Never in my life had I ever been more intimidated, nor would I ever be more so than I was in that moment. After a couple seconds of activity, silence fell upon everybody, they just sat and waited for us to begin. My entire mind went numb, I couldn't think, my arms felt weak, useless. My fingers were noodles and I wasn't sure if I'd even be able to play.

In. Out. Cool, ocean air passed through my lungs, I focused on the air chilling my bare chest. My hair now reached passed my shoulders and I focused on the ends tickling my back, I'm a person, just me, none of these other people's opinions mattered, it was time to do what I was supposed to do, what I knew I should do since that trip that felt like a lifetime ago.

I played the intro of "Paint it Black", paused, and Drew followed with the drums and you could just feel the energy exploding from the whole stage as each instrument melded together. Here we were, playing in an amphitheater dedicated to one of my heroes (although not legally playing there, but those are just little details), and we were playing with over a thousand people dancing and having an amazing time. Just over a year ago I thought I was destined to be a beach bum and take over Skip's shop, but within a matter of weeks and after few random events, my fate changed entirely. I was out there making people happy, and I was doing it with music. It hit me then how insane the chain of events leading up to that moment was, but that's where the beauty of it all rested..

Next up was mine and Drew's favorite Led Zeppelin song. The moment we started to lay down the intro to "Immigrant Song", Feather let out a shout that pierced the very air around us that melded with the wind and was carried around the city. More and more people began to file in as we played our asses off. Some were noticeably intoxicated or under the influence of various substances, but they were still having a good ass time.

Drew slipped up a bit halfway through the song, but got back into it when I shot him a look of disapproval. With the end of the song I saw him bring his hand to his nose and confirmed what I suspected was his "pick me up", but before I could walk over to talk to him, Laura started to play "St. Stephen". I joined in and we all got back into it, my focus moved from Drew onto the music.

I looked onto each person, I quickly scanned the entire crowd of around 2000 and saw the happiness on each individual's face brought to them by our music. As we neared the end of the song, I went up to Feather and started singing with him, droplets of sweat began creeping down my forehead and then hit the ground as the ending solo came on. After this I was really feeling something fast, crazy, something we hadn't played before and nobody was expecting us to play. While racking my brain, I heard some extremely drunk guy in the front shout "Let's hear some Van Halen you hippies!" As they say in my awful job, the customer is always right, so Drew and I made eye contact knowing exactly what to play and put down the intro for "Hot for Teacher" (not before downing a beer offered by the drunk).

I was bouncing around stage, wailing on the guitar like I never had before, my hair flying everywhere, getting up next to Ethan and joining in on the chorus, sliding across stage and making direct eye contact with this gorgeous brunette in the crowd. Normally I don't like girls with shorter hair, but this one fuckin rocked it! An amazing body and frosted tips, she was goin' crazy to the song, and when she realized I was looking at her, she gave me a little wink. I went right into a solo afterwards and played like I'd never played before.

The female figure most definitely has some sort of magical power, given it made me play like I did in that moment. I knew what I was doing after the show. In that moment I knew that I was a fucking rockstar. Rock was back and I was not just at the forefront of that revival, but I was playing guitar with the man who was that revival.

"I really hope you filthy apes enjoyed that right there, but ya know what, we're gonna slow it down a bit, you've heard stuff other people have made, but now's about time for a little somethin we've done ourselves. Just so you guys know, we're not really officially allowed to be here, so if anybody too official looking shows up, could ya do us a favor and block the path best you can so we can get a headstart," Feather said, unnerving half the crowd and exciting the other half, a perfect blend of emotions, that compliment each other like nothing else can.

Feather led off with a laid back song about the beach and surfing, something I wasn't quite ready for, but I did what I could to match the chords I was playing with with his vocals, but I'd never played anything resembling surf guitar before, so midway through I stopped trying to emulate Los Straitjackets and just played what I want, which came out sounding like the dead, but it didn't feel quite right so I just mixed the two and something came out that I hadn't heard before, but really, really liked. Drew and Laura each were doing their own thing, and by the end of the song, we'd melded our sounds together perfectly and just kept playing even after Feather finished. He started doing another song he wrote; it was the story of a trip he had that he crafted into a comment on today's completely bogus political buttfuck we call a government (those last six words taken straight from the man's mouth). Three fourths of the way through I got an opportunity to just play as I please and played a solo that more than outdid the one I had while we were covering Van Halen.

Thing is, I just kept going, and going and going and going til I could barely go anymore. My fingertips got close to bleeding and I ended on one last strum. That's when I realized two things, the first being at least ten minutes had passed since I started my solo, and the second being there was a bit of panic in the crowd, and not the good kind either. I'm talking the "There's very official looking dudes comin' down through the crowd" kind of panic, and personally, and I genuinely dislike that kind of panic, so we grabbed our gear and booked it off the stage. Within minutes we were back at the Travelin' Trouble Machine and on our way back to the apartment.

"Why are we goin' home? All we'll do is lay around, maybe get shconed, and then fall asleep and we could do the same thing tomorrow! Let's fuckin do something guys!" Drew said, obviously a bit anxious for an adventure.

"I dunno, that was pretty tiring. I'm ready to go meditate," Feather responded.

"Ethan, you need to get out more than any of us, I'm leaving it up to you, but you know you want to go have a good time!" Drew said.

"Come on Feather, don't be a pussy! Drew's right, you've done nothing but meditate and write songs, you rarely even come surfing. I'm honestly worried, you need to get out," Laura added.

"Fine, we're going out! But we have to be back by 1am at the latest!" Feather said, succumbing to the peer pressure (although it was the truth).

"Laura, text a few of the regulars and let's see

where the party is tonight! I'm sure that after that, we can get in anywhere we want," I said with a grin on my face. I said it before and I'll say it again, we were fuckin rockstars.

AMERICAN WOMAN

So it was about 2am, an hour later than Feather planned on going home, and he was partying with no sign of stopping. At that point in time I was at around twelve shots and two bowls, and I know that Feather was well over seventeen shots and had smoked more than most do in their entire lives when the cops came to shut down the house party we were at.

"Oi! Fuck right off piggies! We're just havin' a good time! Also, do you guys know where the bathroom is?" Feather blurted out, his drunken, slurred speech was barely comprehensible.

"Calm down or you're coming with us kid! It's 2am, you guys better shut down right now!" one of the officers said.

Everybody but Feather did what's normally done in that sort of situation and ran out. The neighbor's fence was knocked down in the process, and I grabbed a beautiful bong on my way out that somebody just left sitting around on the table.

Behind me was a trail of destruction. Drew and Laura were ahead of me. I could hear a lot of profanities and one of the cops yelling, and I knew exactly where Feather was.

See, Feather never was really ever belligerent or anything of the such, but if you give that guy copious amounts of alcohol in addition to whatever else he might've taken that night, well, then Feather takes a complete 180 and turns into a party animal. Party Feather takes shit from nobody whatsoever, and the only authority he has is himself. He purposely makes stupid decisions just to show he can, which is actually how he ended up in the back of a police cruiser and later a cell, but I didn't find any of that out til the morning after.

Normally I would've been chasing after that cruiser with Feather in the back of it, but I was preoccupied with people who saw us live from earlier that day. People swarmed around Laura, Drew, and I once the chaos had subsided. We promptly decided to continue the party outside and we all marched towards downtown San Francisco. There was about 100 of us, drunk out of our minds, and waltzing around the near deserted streets acting as though we owned them before finding a beach to keep partying on.

"You there! That's my fucking bong you dick!" I heard an extremely drunk girl shout.

Since It was a female, I resisted every urge I would normally have to run with the amazing glass, and my dick started doing my thinking and told me to turn around.

"Sorry! Saw it there and grabbed it, you want it back?" I responded, and that's when I saw her. The same girl I saw earlier that day in the crowd was walking towards me. What are the chances that the bong I took was hers?

"Of course I do, dipshit! Wait, I know you, do you play guitar for that band who was playing at the Jerry Garcia Amphitheater?" she asked.

"Yep! We're called Euphoric Blue, here's your bong back, sorry again," I said as I handed back the bong.

"Oh my god! I'll smoke you the hell out! You guys were amazing! And that solo you did at the end, were you on something?"

"Haha! I wish I was, but honestly I was way too nervous, that's the biggest show we've ever done! It was also the first time we did our own songs. Normally we just do covers, but our front man, Feather, is fucking insane. Freak-of-nature decided to do something original in that moment."

"Damn, didn't really see like it, do you guys have any albums out?"

"Not yet, I don't think anybody would buy any!"

"Are you kidding me? I bet each and every person there would buy at least one copy of anything you guys put out! The energy you guys put in was insane. I can't even begin to explain how dope that was! I don't think I ever introduced myself, though, I'm Ali."

"Kevin, so how about that smoke?"

"I know an awesome spot."

I woke up that morning on top of a hill on and under blankets that came from, well I have no idea where they came from. None of that mattered. All I cared about was the gorgeous girl laying down on my chest. I could barely even remember the night before and after leaving the party. It was basically all hazy until the amazing sex I had on top of the grassy hill, and then I remember watching the stars and acting like I knew the constellations. I wonder where everybody else was... Drew and Laura must be off wherever the party ended up and Feather... Feather was... oh no...

"Holy shit! Feather is in jail!" I exclaimed.

"Wait... what?" Ali responded, groggy as I just

woke her up.

"The singer from my band, Feather! Ethan Feather! I remember last night seeing him in the back of a police cruiser after the cops shut down the party. Where would they have taken him?" I asked.

"Um, I'm not sure. I can think of where a police station is and I-" Ali began to say.

"Take me there now!" I finished and jumped up and realized I was stark naked. "Shit! Ali... where's our clothes?"

"It looks like they blew down the hill," she said and I began to sprint down the hill, naked as the day I was born.

It was honestly amazing, running down that hill at full speed with nothing between myself and the world. Well, right up until I tripped and rolled and rolled and rolled, and that's when I realized why clothes were so crucial. I got up and my whole body was itchy, and even places I never thought could get that kind of itchy. Worst of all, friction burns, friction burns on places you definitely don't want them. I won't go too much into detail, but I can tell you that goddamn, great things are really good at turning to complete shit, but with Ali walking down the hill naked as I was, I realized that there's always good following the bad, and, goddamn, this was surely something good.

We got dressed and went on our way, I lost my shoes, but I don't even know if I had them since the show. The entire time we walked I couldn't get over just how beautiful she was, and I decided to make today something she'd remember beyond "I got fucked by some guitarist and helped him pick his lead singer up from jail" (although that is something very memorable). I wanted to make today even better than

67

the previous night's sex. As soon as we were close to the station, I thanked her for showing me the way and I suggested we go on a bit of an adventure. Knowing no adventure was complete without the aid of something magic, I pulled out a small bag of shrooms.

"Holllld on, I've never ever done anything beyond smoking some weed before," Ali said.

"Oh damn you really need to take these then! Trust me when I say this though, it's much more than bright colors, most of it's in your head. The thought process is the trippy part," I said.

"But I also don't fuckin' wanna go crazy!" she exclaimed.

"Are you kidding me? You don't go crazy from shrooms! The reason people got 'fried' was through constant abuse. Like more than once a week use of high doses for an extended period of time, but even then you don't go insane, you get what's called HPPD. But, people did go crazy from an acid imposter with a side effect of psychosis that was only on the street because the real and safe thing is illegal. You know shrooms are less harmful than acid, and that's less harmful than weed, which is less harmful than Advil. Shit is sideways as all hell," I ranted and rambled.

"So I'm not going crazy after this?" she asked obviously confused by my jumbled answer.

"Well, you probably are already, but aren't we all?"

"Quit with your hippy shit and let's just trip!"

So about an hour later we were going through the wharf and having an amazing time. We got matching pairs of quality, ten dollar, gas station sun glasses to hide our dilated pupils as we went through the city.   There was a small aquarium there that was just insanely awesome, I looked at the fish and they looked at me. I stared the creatures directly in the eyes, I knew somebody was home. Goodness gracious, these things are alive! Alive like me, like Ali, goodness she's gorgeous look at her.   I've never seen anybody so fascinated with life.

"Oh my god they're alive, and they think and they're just like us!" she exclaimed.

"I know! I'm just realizing it! They're more than 'just fish' they live their own life! Just like the people around us.   They have their own thoughts. Think how amazing it is we have thoughts that we think on our own, independently, nobody thinks like me and nobody thinks like you and nobody thinks like him or him or her and oh my god, you're fucking gorgeous!" I crazily explained.

Psychedelics, they're something else.   They allow you to not just think about thinking, but think about thinking about thinking about thinking about thinking while simultaneously fully examining the human condition and its relation to that of every other life-form and the interconnectedness of each and every organism, not just with each other, not just with the planet, Mother Earth, but with the entire universe and whatever force, entity, energy, god(s), or goddess(es) make up everything. The best part is, not only can you think about it, you can connect, fully and truly connect with it all. You can connect like I talked about before, and you can just, you can just be everything because you are everything, and everything is you. Yin is yang, and yang is yin, and they're both yin and yang. They're the individual and the whole, just as everything is, just as we all are, just as- OH MY GOD LOOK AT ALI'S

ASS.

Looking at her ass through my peepin' poppers, I realized how insane it is to have peepin' poppers. The fact that these eyeballs evolved into my friggin' eye sockets is pure insanity. Like, the chain of events leading to me and three people playing a show in front of 2000 people is outrageously complex and just totally unlikely, but the chain of events leading to the development of our eyes... my goodness. the shit that went down over millions of years for those eyes to happen and then even more random events had to take place for other random events to take place for a man to meet a woman to make babies and one of those babies was Ali who had to have every random event in her life happen to get her to the point where she'd go to a concert and happen to look at me at the right time so my brain could register her. THEN, after all of that she had to be at the same party that I decided to go to after my own respective random chain of events to lead me to the point of the party, and then I had to make the decision to take her bong and she had to decide to follow the crowd to find another party over going home. It's fucking nuts, and it all led to me staring directly at her ass on shrooms in an aquarium. Thank you evolution.

But, what's even more insane is the unchanged predators swim, swim, swimmin' around the aquarium. How in the hell does something evolve to be such an efficient predator that it survives some of the craziest mass extinctions **AND** the total and the complete assfucking of the environment by the military industrial complex that us humans are so fond of. The price of our tendency to want the shiniest penny around has brought the death of numerous lifeforms, and brought many more to the brink of extinction and beyond. Like seriously, "WHAT THE FUCK GUYS!" I exclaimed as the thoughts being thought in my head leaked out of my big gaping facehole. Multiple heads turned to make their seeingholes fix upon the profanities being yelled from my fleshy bonesack of a body.

"Kevin! Calm down! They're gonna know, unless, shit is everybody else tripping? They don't care, they're tripping too! Shit if they're all tripping, what does that make us! Kevin does that mean we're sober? Kevin we've got to get out of this place if we're the only sober ones! Those fuckin hippies will kill us on their crazy hippy drugs!" Ali said, panicking more than I think any human being should panic.

"Ali! Chill, you know these fuckers aren't tripping, we are! We're the crazy hippies on the crazy hippy drugs who are going to kill the Sober Sallies! We have to leave before we do because that's just not nice. Do you have any idea what kind of things had to happen for them to get to this point? Think about eyes, Ali, they're insane and we can't just poke them out! Let's just... let's just go... OH MY GOD WE CAN PET STINGRAYS, WE'RE GOING TO GO PET THOSE STINGRAYS!"

It took us about three hours to do so, but we ended up in Berkeley, and we got there while peaking. In all honesty the only reason we had to go to Berkeley was we could sneak onto and off Bart because Ali knew a guy, but that's more than a good enough reason for me. I've done stupider, crazier, riskier things for less. Those things were funny as hell, though, especially the pepper spray in my ass. Pure fucking comedy.

Anyway while in Berkeley we decided to go to some venue that used to be crazy big back when punk bands were springing up left and right in the Bay. I'm talkin the Dead Kennedys, later Rancid, and finally, Green Day (AKABM punk's death rattle). The venue did mostly hardcore bands, rap, and electronic music now, but that was beside the point as nobody was playing at the time, so we did what any rational person on lots of drugs would do and we broke in to wander around.

"What in fuck's name are you guys doing here! How the hell did you get in!" said a short, fat man as he began to scream at us.

"Sorry, uh, sir. We-we, uh, we found an unlocked door and just wandered in. Sorry, we just thought it'd be cool, I'm really sorry. I'm just in this band with some friends and I thought it'd be cool to just look around and, uh, day dream a bit," I sputtered out in response.

"Hold on, are you that dude who plays guitar for those guys who blasted music through LA a while back? One of my employees showed me a video of you guys back then and showed me some article this morning of you guys playing at Jerry's Amphitheater," the man said.

"As a matter of fact, I am that dude! Good to meet you man, well we gotta, uh, go," I said with insane mushroom-fueled thoughts running through my mind. Talking to this squat, little man was far above my pay grade at that moment. That and, he was aiming to kill me, nobody was that bald without extreme homicidal tendencies (or so psilocybin had convinced me).

"Hold on! I won't do anything about the

broken window or the fact you're trespassing if you get your band to play here in a week! You can sell whatever merch you want, but ticket sales go 100% to me, and I'm not paying you guys a dime to show up. That's mostly because I have a feeling you'd pay it back to get the window fixed. Door-in-the-back-was-unlocked my ass! One week from today at 6 o'clock! I see you getting big, if you decide to stop being a drugged up hippy. You're unique, you're opening for some shitty ass band so people will say to themselves 'wow, those openers were actually better, let's check em out' and buy your goddamn CDs up, and I get 15% of those CD sales as well. I better see you there, but until then, I want you outta my fuckin sight!" he finished, leaving myself and Ali confused as to what had just happened, but we both came to the conclusion that it's probably a good thing we're playing.

It didn't matter how mad he actually was in the end, because a week from now, we'd be playing on his stage... wait... less than a fuckin week! Time was already ticking and we had to have a CD by then! I needed Feather for that...

"I'm leaving to get Feather, this is urgent! We NEED to make an album, we gotta go now!" I said in a panic, realizing each second counted.

"Relax man, just chill for a bit!" Ali responded.

"Hell no! I have to! That's the reason behind this trip, we didn't end up here by chance! We have to go, and I need to get Feather!"

Within what felt like seconds we were back on BART, and then we were with Feather. He got released about three hours before and was just sitting on the concrete steps, thinking and figuring out what to do. Ali left when I started approaching him and I never had another conversation with her again, saw her around a bit, but never again would I talk to her.

"Kevin! We need to record an album! Think of how many people were there yesterday, that was amazing!" Feather said.

"One step ahead of you, man. That girl, Ali, and I went on some insane trip and ended up in Berkeley. We broke into some venue, can't remember the name, but I can remember the building and how to get there... kinda... maybe I just need to trip when we play there to find it," I rambled, Feather perked up.

"Wait what? Play there? Kevin... did you get us booked at a real venue?" Feather asked.

"Oh, ya I did. We also need to have a CD made, and a buncha copies of said CD that we can sell," I answered.

"Kevin... how are we gonna make a buncha CDs between now and then?!?"

"Easy! I've got enough money to buy a computer that we can put some mixing software on. We already have some recording equipment, but we can complete what we need by having everybody pool money together!"

"Well shit, we've gotta get on that then!" Feather finished, and with that, we began our walk back to our studio apartment, this was the first time either of us had a chance to make a name for ourselves, and shit, we were gonna make one hell of a name.

74

Break on Through (To the Other Side)

The headlining band had just finished the show and we were selling our CDs. In that one week span, Drew, Laura, and I all quit our jobs and the whole band spent 12 hours a day recording and recording. We produced one CD of 14 covers and another of 10 original songs. The first five we played nonstop, one after the other and did the same for the next five. We recorded each grouping multiple times and put the best recording in each spot, unless it messed with the flow.

Feather and mine's vision for the album was to not only have it be good and send a message, all of that jazz, but to flow and really tell a story. Nowadays music comes out and each song is designed to be either all out amazing or filler, but we put the same amount of effort in each song, crafted a story, an entire journey, and we did it through music. In the end it was really just two long songs, each having short breaks between a series of five parts, but it all flowed. It was a book and each song was a chapter.

The venue was nearly empty when a man approached. He was tall, had slicked back brown hair, and an expensive looking suit on, but I couldn't tell if it was actually nice, as my wardrobe consisted of plain t-shirts and jeans. Although some tie dye would make a good addition and be fun as sh-

75

"You guys had a real nice show, liked your style. It's new. Something nobody's heard before. Name's Brendan Steinberg, and I want to help you guys. There's been a lot of talk down in LA, mostly good stuff, a lot of people are after you guys, lotta scumbags, lotta douches, but I'm here, all the way up here in Berkeley, because I want you guys. I want you guys to be big. The scumbags and the douches, they'll have you guys blow up, but then they'll let you fade away and take their 30, 40, 50, sometimes even 60 percent. I'm only asking for ten percent, I don't want you guys just to be famous, I want your message to be heard and I want real music back, not this shit where an album has three good songs out of 12, or this 'pussy, money, bitches' kinda thing. No, I want real music, a real message. I want something the people of not just this country, but this world can get behind. Something like that, it needs a face, and it needs a voice. Euphoric Blue is both of those. Anybody can get behind this, hell I bet you the geezers can with the way you trade off on solos or your freestyled-when-live-lyrics because it may have the face of rock 'n' roll, but it's got the soul of jazz," Brendan finished. The guy talked extremely fast, and he sounded real scripted until about halfway through when it was noticeable that he was putting real thought, real emotion, real soul behind what he was saying. He truly believed in his words and he truly believed in us.

"Sorry man, but I don't want to be famous. I like this," Feather said before any of us could respond.

"What?" the agent replied.

"I don't want to be famous and I don't want any money. I don't want any of that. Look, you can sell our music if you want, but I don't want my face, myself attached to it. You can give the other three all the money or keep my share yourself, I don't want to be famous, I just want my message to be heard," Feather finished.

All of us, Lauralyn, Steinberg, Drew, and myself, all stood there in shock. Seeing Feather, the man who would be our leader if we had one, deny the opportunity of a lifetime.

"Well, if you want your message to be heard, you still have to come down to LA with me," Brendan said, not even phased by the denial of his offer.

"One condition, you sign this," Feather scribbled something down on a piece of paper, "It says you keep half my share of the money on top of your ten percent, and the band retains full creative process of all the music produced."

"That's more than fair, no problem!" Steinberg replied, signing his name, "Here's the address, be down there no later than a week."

About an hour later the whole band was out in the water, the only light was provided by the full moon. It was one last surf in Pacifica as residents of San Francisco. Leaving the city that had become the closest thing to a home (other than the Travelin' Trouble Machine of course) any of us had was equal parts heartbreaking as it was exciting. Well over a year had passed since we settled down and began honing our musical skills, each of us had become restless and I knew Feather had to be on the road to get more life experience for more stories, for more songs, and, most importantly, for more fun.

"Let's get back quick, we'll harvest the garden, take all the seeds we can, pack up anything we want to bring, and be off," Feather said, more anxious than anybody to get behind the wheel.

It took only an hour to grab our few belongings, most of which were put in a small trailer solely for storage that the TTM would lug on our journey. To our surprise, Feather headed north rather than south when he began driving.

"Feather, where in the hell are you going?" said a buzzed Drew.

"North, I want to explore Vancouver Island before settling down again. Between studio time and possible tours, I may never get a chance to do so again," Feather answered as he really began to accelerate.

The drive was long and tedious, by the time we reached our destination, a small house next to a dock and a large boat in northern Washington, we were all tired and hungry. It was good for Drew, we found his stash of blow and sold it for some money for food, forcing him to go cold turkey for the following few days. On the third day without his crutch, his withdrawals were at their worst. Drew looked like absolute shit, and it was obvious he felt worst than he looked, so I did with him what I remember my dad doing with my brother while going through the same thing. We fished.

I don't remember much of him, but my brother was a really nice, friendly guy. He was nine years older than me and used to be an amazing running back until he got into heroin. It all began with a prescription for Oxycontin after surgery on his shoulder, and he became much too fond of it. Eventually his habit brought him to bankruptcy so he switched to smack, a much cheaper alternative. During his senior year, his performance on the field began to lag far behind what it could've been. He got skinny, slower, and angry. Scouts lost their interest in him although that was high before he fucked himself over. The sociable, kind man I knew had turned into a timid, angry boy focusing solely on his next fix. Not too long after, he dropped out of school, the only time I saw him around was when he was asking my dad for money, and once my dad stopped giving him money, he'd stop by when he couldn't find a couch to crash on, and he'd sleep in the side yard, right next to the trash cans. At 19 my dad helped him quit, they'd fish, he took him to California and Skip taught him to surf, things were looking up, until he got back home and he was back on smack thanks to his friend Theo. It only took two more weeks for him to finally overdose, and, poof, my brother was gone. I don't blame heroin for the loss of my family member, I blame Oxycontin. I blame the doctors who overprescribe those medications. I blame the people pushing the lab grade heroin onto teenagers and ruining their lives for a fucking profit.

As the thoughts of my brother passed, I sat with Drew for a couple hours in complete silence. We just enjoyed nature, and it was the first time in a while I saw a smile matched by a look in his eyes that sent the same message. Even though we only caught two small trout, it was probably one of the best days fishing I can remember.

Drew didn't quit coke after that. We got to LA not much after and he was back on it, but it gave his mind and body the break it needed. Drew could once again be our drummer.

The recording studio was surreal and made me realize how far we'd come in such a short amount of time. I was supposed to be working register in a surf shop, but instead I was in a quality recording studio with Botox junkies with spray tans, and each with their very own gold digger of a wife. Steinberg was present for the first and the last recording sessions, but between those he partied and he partied hard. This man entering the age that most begin their midlife crises, was partying harder than anybody I'd ever seen. Being without a family meant Steinberg was without responsibilities, and without responsibilities he could do more blow in a sitting than how much our producer smoked in a week.

I realized that everybody did some sort of drug in LA. A select few including myself, Feather, and Laura liked our psychedelics, almost everybody smoked weed, and any person you saw walking around with a suit on probably had a bump of coke in the past hour. It made the city seem as though it was running smoothly, but crumble from the base up. The people living on the streets sold their shit to the people living in the mansions, allowing them to have enough money to support themselves off of dealing as long as they like, until they have a family, and then they need more money. The problem is when somebody who has sold drugs their whole life needs more money, they can't get a conventional job, so they have to get some shit pay minimum wage job and continue dealing on the side if they want to support those they love.

Now, Mr. Bigshot sitting in his suede suit and on the studio's leather couch could still buy his blow to get him to and fro, while his buddy at Wells Fargo could lobby so that it's to jail their street dealer is destined to go. It shouldn't be that way, I wish I could say it wasn't so, but that's just the way life goes, and now that dealer is in jail his daughter is going to have some daddy issues like the rest of the hoes, and with her body up for sale, Bigshot can buy an hour before going back to work.

It shouldn't be this way but it's not the opinion of Mr. Bigshot I need to sway. Its that of those hating others simply because they're gay, straight, liberal, or conservative with no reason other than that's what their preacher preaches before passing around a tithe to pay. It shouldn't be this way, playing life like it's a game and using others as pawns. It's honestly a great big shame and, if I say so myself, quite a fucking sham. Hell, they've got guys on TV trying to take advantage of your goddamn gam gam, and there's nothin you can do about it, but shit, if it's the last thing I do, Mr. Bigshot and the rest of his friends are gonna be paying taxes too.

"Feather! Come here!" I shouted excitedly.

"What is it?" he asked running over.

"I've got an idea for a song..." and that's how I wrote my first song.

Two weeks later and after a lot of begging, ass kissing, and everything in between, our song was getting played on three different radio stations, and after another two weeks three more hopped on the bandwagon and we made the top 40. Not too long after we released a real, studio recorded album with sound quality that was actual quality, and by that I mean it didn't sound like it was recorded in some goddamn studio apartment by four tripping hippies trying to save themselves from what could only be called salary slavery. Now that we had something worth really releasing in a music store near you, I'd finally realized my dream, my goal, had come true. We were making a difference under the now known name of Euphoric Blue.

Within three months we'd released four singles and an album, and that was just beginning. LA was insane. Every morning I woke up and each day I was afraid in all the money and craziness I'd lose my way. Feather was a leader, he could get shit done, but while Laura was out with whatever model or hollywood actor had asked her out that night, and Drew was out partying with whatever C and B list rappers he was partying with that night, Feather had nobody to keep him company while he sat around and powered through an extra large pizza and watch whatever movie he felt like watching that night. I wasn't surprised by his love for fantasy, as the vast universe containing Middle Earth is something I imagine he could think up on a five day drug binge (as that's the kind of thing he did think up of, he plotted out an entire series of nine fantasy books, complete with its own pantheon and history in a two week long LSD binge. Redosing each time he began to come down. Feather never stopped writing, not even to sleep during that 2 week period), but what was surprising was his love of war movies. I'd expect Feather to get sad and angry that kind of shit happened in real life, which he did, but he also got excited at the violence. He straight went nuts every time something crazy and badass happened that ended with a bunch of people getting blown up. That's when I first noticed the wild side to the seemingly laid back singer.

During this period, Feather began experimenting with different kinds of music he hadn't heard before. Although he despised rap, he listened to some of the original rappers from way back and became entranced. Next was metal beginning with Black Sabbath, then Metallica, then Slayer, and then he went down the rabbit hole into the countless different genres. Shit, Feather found shepherd metal, metal dedicated to the subject of shepherding. It was all about fucking sheep (quite literally in multiple songs actually). Finally, Feather found punk again. He'd listened to it back before leaving home, but now he was older and much wiser, the same songs sounded completely different to the same pair of ears their sound waves penetrated a few years prior.

Now that we enjoyed a life of doing whatever the fuck we wanted for a couple months thanks to the revenue of our now popular music, we decided to head back to the studio. Drew and Laura looked like shit, I'd just surfed, and Feather, well shit Feather had disappeared for a minute there. He came back and his hair was a little bit messier than normal, which was strange to see as I didn't think that was possible. Feather's hair was about as long as mine now, it looked like he got a couple inches cut and it fell just below his shoulders. Drew had bags under his eyes and cocaine to match under his nose. Laura just seemed like she'd been in a car accident and smelled like stale smoke, booze, and sex.

Laura and Drew's hangovers did not surprise me, but Feather's, goodness, I was not ready for him to be hungover. He dragged his feet up to the microphone and grabbed my guitar. He told Steinberg and Mr. Bigshot we were doing something totally different this time around.

"Start recording... you bitches," he mumbled.

83

The light came on and Feather began muttering profanities into the microphone, ones I knew and ones that I think he made up on the spot- as one does while hungover and simultaneously drunk. Feather began pacing before tripping over a chord, flat on his face. He proceeded to yell really fuckin' loud, and then he started shouting the lyrics of "My War" by Black Flag into the microphone. He started doing what he always does and began to just sing whatever popped into his mind. Normally his lyrics meant something, but this time around they were very violent, rebellious, and nonsensical.

The first song we did was about fighting, the next about drinking, and the third about drinking and fighting. I didn't agree one bit with the music, as none of it was really my forte, but I did what I could to match my bandmates in following Feather's lead. Playing guitar for the style of music Feather was singing was simple. All power chords and nothing too complicated, and shit I didn't even have to solo. Guitar was my way to be free and share myself with the world, and Feather was getting in the way of this.

By the time we finished recording this punk album, a month had passed, and unlike what we normally do, the songs were recorded individually. Feather shaved his head and began taking me with him to the underground shows he frequented. Each show was the same: insanely high energy, violence, and a giant mosh pit. The more I studied Feather at the concert, the more I realized he was revolted by the lyrics, which confused me because he spent every weekend in some abandoned warehouse or garage listening to these bands.

"Ethan... what the fuck are you doing?" I asked after the show.

"What do you mean?" Feather responded.

"You've totally flipped around, you went from the dirtiest dirty hippy I know to a punk partying day and night, the music you're making isn't the music you make dammit!" I shouted, releasing all the pent up rage from the past month of torturous recording sessions.

"Isn't it beautiful?" Feather said in a way that reminded me of the guy I know.

"Not really, that album was complete trash and it's not Euphoric Blue. It's not us!" I responded.

"That's the point! We can do whatever we want. We don't have to always make the same kind of music. Shit, if we wanted we could do raps to heavy metal and broadway style vocals during the chorus. Kevin, we have full creative control and that's what this proved."

"But you're not acting like yourself, Feather, this isn't you. It's not about creative control, it's about you coming in hungover all the time which justifies Lauralyn's partying and Drew's blow problem. You're the glue keeping this band together and we're falling apart just as we're getting big."

"Well shit that would suck if we fell apart."

"Feather! We are falling apart!"

"No, Kevin, you are."

"But we're a family, Ethan, and that's what made this so great, Now it's all just... it's just shit now. I can't remember the last time we all spent quality time together!"

"We never fuckin' were a family," Feather finished as he lit a cigarette and walked away, leaving me alone with the faint, pungent odor of his stoge.

Not knowing what to do, I texted my drug plug and within minutes my dealer, Kerouac, was outside the old warehouse that the band had turned to a venue. Kerouac and I went back a bit. He had lived in San Diego and I first met him through Drew. We liked each other so much back in the day, we tried setting his mom up with Skip, but that obviously never worked out. Every time he went on his monthly run up to Mendocino, he'd stop by our loft in San Francisco and smoke me out. Guys like Kerouac, they're hard to find. They're genuine about most everything they do, and like just about anybody and everybody, except those who are fake and not acting as they actually are. We obviously kept in touch, and, thankfully, he had moved to the City of Angels a week before I did.

"Are you okay, man?" he said pulling up in his tiny Fiat.

"It's just Feather, he's been an ass lately. I have no idea what to do, the whole band has fallen apart. Lauralyn can barely play bass anymore since she's spending too much time drinking, smoking, and whatever the hell else she does. All Drew does anymore is snort coke and pound whiskey... Feather... fucking Ethan has turned completely punk and shit, we're not even making music anymore," I said.

"What do you mean? Your guys' new album is doing really well with all the punks. I was just at this party and they decided to play the album and it was pretty solid, for punk," Kerouac said.

"But, that's not us, that's not Euphoric Blue," I said as I climbed into shotgun. The car danked like no other. Two thick joints sat on the center console, both calling my name.

"Look man, we've all got our vices. Drew's is

coke, Laura's is drinking, and it looks like Feather's is not giving a shit. People like me and you, shit we smoke more weed than anybody should. This isn't smoking to enjoy, face it, you smoke just to smoke. To fill the time til you die in an attempt to not get too bored, but you'll always be bored while you're sober and that's why you smoke, and when you smoke, you'll never be more than content. Who are we to judge other people on what they use to fill their time before it's used up?" Kerouac said.

"But this is different, man. The band is falling apart! It's affecting more people than just Feather, and he doesn't realize that."

"So?"

"So?!? If there's no band, then there's no reason for any of this, and I'll just end up some bum! Some fuckin beach bum! Feather has this message he wants to spread, but, if the band falls apart, nobody will hear his voice, change won't come, and we'll all be fucked!"

"We're all already fucked. The moment we're born we're destined to die, and you're right, there's no reason for any of it. None of this has any sort of reason, and that's what's beautiful."

"Beautiful? How can nothing be beautiful?"

"That's for you to find out. I've got some shroomies for you. Eat 'em and turn off your phone. Text me in the morning after your trip ends and tell me why the fact nothing matters is the most important thing there is, why it's beautiful, why this is all beautiful. I'm expecting that text at eight thirty exactly, that gives you thirty minutes to come up and eight hours to trip, now get out and go fuckin' fix this, fix Euphoric Blue if you genuinely think it's broken,"

87

Kerouac said as he handed me a bag containing what looked to be about six grams of shrooms. I ate them all, got out of the car, and then began my journey.

Those shrooms most definitely had very high concentrations of psilocybin, and the potent weed I'd smoked added to the psychedelic concoction being mixed around in my big ol' brain. First place I went was a coffee shop. Psychedelics gave me energy, but weed made me tired so I drank a cup of coffee... did I? I got a second cup and realized I'd already had one, but I had this second cup and I couldn't waste this cup because only people who are waste are wasteful, so I downed it and threw it in the trash, where the cup began its journey to the ocean. Oh my goodness this hit me fuckin' hard.

The kaleidoscope vision was more intense tonight than I'd ever experienced. Everything I looked at was a kaleidoscope with kaleidoscopes inside the larger kaleidoscope and it just got smaller and smaller until infinite before getting bigger and bigger beyond measure. When you perfectly line up two mirrors, you can witness the same effect of infinite, and the infinite I was looking at was everywhere. There was no escape from everything. It was all of time, all of space in this narrow tunnel going forever downwards.

I stumbled out of the coffee shop, receiving weird looks from all the hobbits that were there too. I didn't realize that hobbits drank Starbucks, I saw them more as Pete's people, or maybe as those that would go to independent coffee shops (it was common knowledge that hobbits were hipsters). The goblins across the street on the other hand, looked like they knew how to party.

"'Scuse me, are you king of the goblins? I have a request I'd like to make," I asked the largest one.

"The fuck are you talking about, I'm no goblin!" the goblin king replied, obviously in the middle of some sort of identity crisis.

"My apologies sir, I didn't realize you hadn't looked in a mirror recently because you are most definitely a goblin, and you definitely are their king," I said.

"The hell are you talking about?" the goblin king asked.

"Well obviously you're a goblin, and given that you're fatter, taller, uglier, and much smellier than all these other goblins, that means you must be the goblin king!" I explained to the extremely agitated goblin king, who wasn't taking my compliments well.

I experienced a lapse of consciousness, obviously the goblin king had some sort of memory wiping magic, because I was on the ground and the goblin king and his royal goblin guard had vanished. That left me on an empty sidewalk being laughed at by the hobbits, who had whatever reason to gawk at my predicament. I remembered I was on shrooms, and turned my phone back on, which was hard to do since it had turned into a bar of soap and kept slipping and sliding from one hand to the next. Eventually the phone turned on, but the bountiful bamboozling bamboozlers completely boombazled me (as is their job), but I'd have a greater appreciation for said bamboozling bamboozlers if they'd decided to refrain from boombazzling me in my time of strife, as this was not the proper time to be boombazzled, bamboozled, swtatakoozled, or confused!

I made my way to a large park. How? I don't know. Either ten years or ten minutes had passed, I wasn't sure, but somebody began to play "Comfortably Numb", or maybe it was my Brian's jukebox playing it. Wait who the fuck is Brian? Is Brian my brain? Brian the brain.

"Hey Brian," I said, using my inside voice.

"What's up Kevin?" Brian responded.

"Not much, Kerouac is trying to get me to answer this question, and I have no idea how to do that."

"Well what's the question? Something about nothing and how it's beautiful, or is it what I want for dinner? I want a steak dinner, you should let Kerouac know. Steak is delicious."

"A steak dinner does sound nice..."

"No Kevin, that's not the question. I was just messing around with you. Dammit why are you such a dumbass? The question is most definitely not being asked to find what you want for dinner. You need to learn the beauty of nothing. Nothing matters, and there is beauty in that."

"Well shit Brian, how do you know that but I don't?"

"You know everything you dumbass, but you just haven't realized it yet. Well, I know everything but you don't."

"That doesn't make any sense."

"You're on lots of drugs Kevin, it doesn't have to."

"Okay."

"I think you have to see what nothing truly is to appreciate its beauty."

"I can't see what nothing is because there's no

nothing. You can't show me nothing!"

"You're right, you have to die to see that, your physical body doesn't have to, but you Kevin, you must die if you want to see what nothing is like."

All of the sudden I was in a magnificent forest, and it was somewhere I hadn't ever been before in my whole life. It was a clearing in a forest, the trees looked normal, yet some were purple, red, even blue. I climbed one, looked out, and saw a sea of blue leaves. Every direction I looked there were trees. The giant forests were everywhere, and there were no signs of civilization at all. I climbed down and took a stroll through the woods and felt like I was being watched. My pace gradually quickened until I was sprinting through the forest, leaping over fallen trees, ducking under branches, leaping across narrow canyons carved by rainbow streams. I tripped and tumbled down a hill. Unscathed, I got back to my feet, climbed a tree, and began running along the branches like I was a psychedelic Tarzan.

On the ground I looked around and saw a bunch of toadstools, but they weren't normal toadstools, they were giant. Standing at about a foot tall each, and their stalks were thick as all hell. I went to go inspect when a voice shouted at me and I realized that it was a village of tiny forest people. Fairies, real fairies!

"Faerie! F-A-E. You're in what they call the Faewilds, a mystical place of magic and creatures beyond belief. In the streams you'll find the Nixies, in the canopy you'll find the Pixies and the Sprites, and the trees house the Figgins and the Faeries. If you're lucky you'll run into Satyrs, or maybe even a Centaur if you go to their plains, but they may or may not try and dismember your body. A few decades ago they had a bout with some real nasty, dark forces, but that's a story for somebody else to tell. The elves may show themselves to you if you summon them. They are your people. Hell, everybody here is your subject. Kevin, you are the Archfae," Brian said.

"How do you know all this Brian?" I asked.

"How do YOU know all this! You're tripping and I'm your brain talking to you, YOUR brain," Brian said before I felt his presence leave again.

I got back to running through the forest before running into a small village of tree people, their ears were pointed and I knew they were the elves. They began to sing happy songs and dance around with me. Standing at only two feet tall, they reminded me of the claymation elves from christmas specials mixed with the dudes in Fig Newton commercials, and they were fuckin' talkin' to me. Talkin' to me, man. We sang and we danced in a little circle before falling on the ground. They called me the Elf King, and they praised me as the High Elf.

Spirits from trees came out to me next, they were made of bark, but some were fleshy and I knew they were the Dryads. The nature spirits took my hand and had me follow them. They brought me before the one known as the Forest King.

"Archfae, I humbly bring myself before you to let you know that the darkness has been driven from your realm. You are free to let your people do as they please," the Forest King said. He was a man of average stature and the only other human that inhabited this strange place. He wore beige pants and suspenders with a white t-shirt and looked as though he was directly from the 1950s. His accent was Irish and his words strung together like a song.

"Good job, man. Um, well, I mean you're king, so just keep doin' what you're doin' I guess. I'm gonna go explore," I responded, not knowing how to respond to a king of this fantastical forest.

"Thank you, I gladly accept your appointment as me to be king. I hope you find whatever you're looking for in your exploration," the Forest King responded.

I barreled through the forest once again until I happened upon a clear pond, so clear and clean I thought it was a portal to the sky. I looked at my reflection in the water that was clearer than the cleanest glass, and I was astounded. I had deer antlers growing from my head and long, bleach-blonde hair with a bare face (I always had some sort of scruff present). I wore only a deerskin kilt and nothing else, not even shoes, and my ears were pointed like those of the elves and all the other creatures I encountered. I focused harder than I previously thought I could focused and called on Brian for some help. I regained my normal appearance. I was butt-ass naked, but the good kind of butt-ass naked. I was butt-ass naked in a place I could be more naked than a newborn. I was the only person here who actually gave a shit. This little realm was in my head, and shit who knows, maybe that realm my head was in was in somebody else's head. Maybe real life was in my head too, but it's fun so I could care less.

I eventually found myself in the same clearing I began in and decided to sit down. Around a month had passed and I'd learned the way of the Faewilds. A mystical realm of magic and myth of which I was not the ruler, but the god. I learned to make myself take the appearance of different creatures as to not startle the

Nymphs, Dryads, Pixies, Nixies, Smurfs, Centaurs, Satyrs, Faeries, Brownies, Sprites, and everything else roaming the forest. I was famous enough in the real world, I didn't want to be just as famous here. Otherwise, I wouldn't have created this realm to escape to.

Wait... this realm to escape to... holy shit I'm tripping on shrooms... where am I in the real world? Shit how do I get out? Am I stuck forever? Holy shit holy shit holy shit this whole place is starting to melt away! No, no, no, no, NO! This is not the Faewilds! I need to get back! Where in the fuck am I? How do I get out? What the fuck is that thin? What in the fuck is going on?!? I hate my life... fuck this... fuck everything... I should just end it all when I fucking can... Who the fuck gives a shit anyway? None of it fucking matters... Why in the hell am I having these thoughts? What the fuck is going on? I thought, screaming in my own head, desperately trying to get Brian's attention, but my attempts to do so were all in vain, as I was trapped in the one place from which there's no escape.

The lovely land of the Faewilds had melted away, and, after the mystical realm dissipated, I was dragged down to a place of hatred and despair. Upon arrival, I felt nothing but pure negativity. I was in a low, low realm. The vibrational frequency was lower than anything I could imagine. I was not a man of god, but I do believe the place I was in was Hell, or at least somewhere very close to it.

There was nothing but the negative in this place. It looked like an eternal, infinite cavern that went on forever ahead of me. The ceiling was about fifteen feet above my head, and everything was a grayish black stone. It wasn't hot. There was no fire or lakes of lava. I didn't see any wandering souls. There was just negativity and an endless cavern accompanying the presence of an evil I can't explain to this day, and that was much worst than any depiction of hell I'd seen prior as it needed hellfire, tortured souls, and lakes of fire to induce a feeling of unholy fear in whoever found themselves there. This place did not need that. The mere action of being in that plane was enough for me to know how awful it was.

I walked down the jagged path, and I wandered for hours. No end to the cave was in sight. There was a feeling of something watching me the entire time, so I challenged it to reveal itself. From behind a rock a demonic alien did, in fact, reveal itself, and then grabbed my shoulders. I felt its claws digging into my flesh as warm, wet blood trickle down my back. I had control of this realm, but this thing had control of me. It looked me directly in my eyes, and I felt nothing but pure fear. There was no other emotion nor any memory where I could remember feeling fear so ferociously fantastic as I felt in that fucking moment.

There was nothing I could do to make it stop, and nothing I did to make it start. The creature hadn't made me scared, but when it looked into my eyes I felt fear, not of the creature, nor of the place, and not even fear of myself. Pure, irrational fear of nothing, and, shit, the idea of nothing didn't even scare me. The fact there was nothing causing the fear intensified the terror, and I felt that fear for all eternity, yet only a second.

The Fear Demon released me and dissipated into thin air. I collapsed onto the ground, gasping for air, but I was unable to breathe. I flipped onto my back, and, instantly, thousands of small rats and spiders flooded from cracks and crevices around the cave, and they crawled all over me. When I knocked one rat off, three more would replace it, and with every spider I smashed, sixty six thousand more stupid spiders streamed from their deceased comrade. Within seconds, I was covered. There was nothing but black and rats. Then they began burrowing.

The rats gnawed at my flesh and carved various cavities through my body, and the spiders made webs and colonies throughout the cave system that had developed. More spiders were born and born, and they kept feeding off my body. The rats burrowed deep, anywhere burrowable was aptly burrowed through. They rapidly reached pregnancy and created countless nests that they tucked away throughout my entire body. Four different rats lived in my head, and much too many made multiple homes up and down my whole body. Their babies started eating the spiders and generations of rats came and went, eating each other when spiders went scarce until starvation satisfied the natural order and the newly established species of Kevin Douglas Hell Rats went extinct.

I laid there trembling for what felt like forever, before I climbed back to my feet and pushed further. I was unscathed, somehow, even though I'd just spent the last day as the breeding ground for rats and spiders.

My next adversary approached and attempted creating control over my character, to which I promptly refused before the new demon stabbed me with its scorpion tail and forced me to look at it. The new demon was taller than the last, and it was greenish brown in color, just like the Goblin King. It's giant white eyes stared directly into me while its tail found itself lodged in my back. Hate's four arms grabbed my body. Its claws dug deeper than the last demon as it tore my whole body apart, leaving only my head that was now impaled on its tail. It forced me to look into its eyes and I felt hatred. Pure and true hatred. None purer could ever be felt. This too lasted an eternity and was just as bad as fear. There was nothing I hated, not the demon, not the place, not myself, but that was all I felt. Normally that would call for panic, but I couldn't panic as then I'd stop hating. So, I kept hating and began hating hate, and my hatred for hate eventually caused the feeling itself to be overcome, and just as my hate phased from existence, the demon did too.

I wandered for a sleepless month, before the final demon appeared. I was frozen in place and could do nothing but watch as it approached me. This demon hid its face behind what looked like a strange, three eyed tiki mask. Twisted horns protruded from the top of its head that rose above the tall mask. The creature was slender and tall with four arms that ended with four long fingers, but instead of having claws like the others, gnashing teeth were at the end of each fingertip.

Rooted to the ground, I had no choice but for the creature to begin consuming me. It began with the arms and legs. It wrapped its fingers around me and I began feeling the very flesh being torn from the bone. It worked its way inwards and up until there was nothing left but a bloodstained skeleton I looked down on standing in the spot I once stood. The arms extended outwards and wrapped themselves around my very soul, bringing me closer and closer to the demon's true mouth. The closer I got the louder the low frequency ring in my ears got, until it was deafening

97

and nothing else could be heard. At the peak of it's sound, my entire being became consumed by a feeling of pure negativity in its last moments. The demon was to consume my very being.

"NO!" I heard Feather's voice shout and instantly I was returned to my skeleton and collapsed on the ground. I laid there with the demon standing above me, the feeling having not subsided, and then it's hellhounds came. They devoured my bones and the feeling got stronger and stronger.

What I felt indescribable, even now. It was not hate. It was not fear. It was not dread. It was the feeling of pure, negativity. Pure evil. Pure evil filled every bit of my being for countless hours. The hellhounds kept coughing my bones up, allowing my skin to regrow, and then devouring me all over again while their master stood by and watched. Then, I saw a blade protrude from the abdomen of the creature. It fell to its knees, and just as the tiki mask began to slip and my savior began to remove their hood, everything vanished. Everything.

Now, I sat alone in existence, purely existing and doing nothing more and nothing less, but while doing so I wasn't "I". Brian had left and I was left echoing my own thoughts around my brain for the entirety of time, so I created the universe, and millions of others. All of space and time ceased to exist and what happened was beyond my comprehension. Every second to ever exist and that had ever existed all happened in the span of a singular moment. All of eternity encompassing an isolated segment in time. Then, just as it began, it ended.

I was back at Skip's somehow with Bob's guitar

laying down at my side.   The smell of fresh coffee filled the air, and, surprisingly, Skip was playing a playlist of various country and bluegrass artists. Feather told me we weren't family, because we weren't; Skip was my family and now I knew that. I accepted it. I accepted that my deceased brother, my father, and my mother, wherever and whoever she was, are all apart of that lovely family too. Feather wasn't the one who was sick, it was me.   My drug use was rampant, and I'd become selfish.   I only thought the band was going under because we did something I didn't want them to do, and I had to smoke an absurd amount of weed to make myself numb to the fact I was the problem.   It was time for me to find a place to exist and to enjoy for a bit before I died.

STARMAN

"Mornin' sunshine," said Skip, a big smile on his face.

"How'd I get here?" I responded.

"Well, I think you ended up on a bus given the bus pass you had. I got a call early this morning saying you were in the police station. They found you laying down, naked, on the beach. What the fuck were you doing? I haven't seen you for years and all of the sudden you're naked on a beach!" Skip said, the first time he ever sounded aggressive towards me.

"Shrooms," I answered.

"Ah, I gotchya now. I had myself a little psychedelic phase too. Was this your first trip?" Skip asked.

"No, but it was definitely my last one," I replied.

"Good, I'm guessing you had quite the night then! Only do 'em til you need 'em is what I've always said. Now, do you wanna go surf? Double overhead today," Skip finished.

Within thirty minutes we were paddling out to waves bigger than the surf shop was tall. The fact something naturally existed so large and powerful was amazing in of itself, but the fact I was paddling out to ride it with Skip, that was a whole other thing. It had been far too long since I'd surfed last, close to a year at this point. Fame had made me lose sight of what I loved. I was playing for money and a bigger name. Feather had his turn to write his music, but now it was mine. Each second I rode one of the huge waves, shooting down the line like a bullet, was a second where I came up with more lyrics. By the end of Skip and mine's session, I'd thought of two new songs, and I rushed Skip to get back so I wouldn't pull a Roy and lose the light now that I'd seen it.

Skip had a girlfriend now, something that was new to me. In all the years I'd lived with that old beach bum, he never brought home any girls, never talked about any girls, or even showed general interest in any girls, but now he had an attractive, kind blonde waiting for him back at the shop. Her name was Erin and the pit bull she had with her made me instantly approve. Nacho was his name and although a pit bull, you would've thought that dog was a shtizu. At first it was terrified of me, but eventually it got used to me and I realized that it didn't know it was a large dog (honestly I don't even know if it realized that it was, in fact, a dog). Nacho thought he was a lap dog and made it near impossible for me to write down any songs. I got the first two done, but after that the words stopped flowing and there was nothing worth showing to anybody left in my head.

I turned on the news, and I was on it. "Rockstar arrested while intoxicated, passed out, and naked in public. He was released early this morning, and nobody knows where he is now."

Great, I thought, *this will surely piss off some of the guys working for the label... oh well, I just hope I get some down time before anybody tries to come down and find me.*

101

And down time was what I got. Two weeks flew by while I did nothing but surf, shape, and write music. I was at absolute peace, and without worries or a spotlight, before Drew eventually came down to check on me. He had a letter to show me, and I had a whole album to show him. Mr. Steinberg wasn't too happy with my antics. Apparently more than just my local station put a story out on my antics, every tabloid in Southern California had talked about me to some extent.

Somebody caught a video me getting punched in the face by a short, fat man who I was thoroughly convinced was the king of all Goblins, but apparently he wasn't. Another video was circulating of me running through a park proclaiming myself Archfae and warden of the Fae wilds before falling down and rolling around the grass in pure euphoria. Between then and getting home I assumed I took a bus where I went to hell and had my ego death experience, and somehow I ended up on a beach. Why I was naked on the beach, I had no idea, but it was big news and nobody involved with the band was happy with it. Although, Feather thought it was absolutely hilarious.

"So, you just had a huge trip, ended up down here, and wrote enough songs for a whole album?" Drew asked.

"Basically. I've done a lot of surfing and I've spent a bunch of time with Skip and his girlfriend who has the cutest fuckin' dog ever. But dude, I think I'm almost ready for recording, but I don't want this one being done with the Hollywood assholes," I answered.

"You're not the only one. Lauralyn bailed, she disappeared after we couldn't find you saying if you

102

were out, she was too. She said we're not making music anymore, we're making money. And it's not even money for ourselves! We're making money for Steinberg and those assholes! I hired a lawyer to read over the contracts, and, aside from the bonuses, we're making jack shit. Steinberg keeps 20 percent of profits himself, his recording studio gets another 50 percent, and that leaves 30 percent for us to split four ways. We got fucked on the fine print. That's why Feather did a punk album. He knew and was trying to get us released from that contract 'cause, unless those assholes say otherwise, Euphoric Blue is on their label until 2018," Drew explained before doing a quick bump of blow.

"Don't do that shit in here, man! But, back to Steinberg, Euphoric Blue is fucked until 2018, but what if we made a new band, with the same members? The Bums aren't stuck in that contract," I responded.

"The Bums?" Drew responded, chuckling.

"The Bums."

"Kevin, Drew, some people are here asking for you two!" Skip shouted.

Drew and I had been living in the back room of the surf shop. I took the couch, he had an air mattress and blankets. We'd spent the past few days doing nothing more than jamming, surfing, and then spearfishing our dinners. It was like back when we were on our road trip so long ago. All our lives were at the time was playing music, surfing, and barbecuing our dinner with Skip's new friends and Erin. We basically had adopted Nacho in the few days Drew had been down. He slept with us in the back room, and we fed him leftovers and cheap dog food.

"Who is it?" I shouted, groggy from being

woken up an hour earlier than I naturally got up.

"Come out here and see for yourself you lazyass!" Skip replied.

I came out and I was met with two faces that were all too familiar. Lauralyn and Ethan Feather were standing before me in Skip's surf shop with big smiles on their faces. It had been weeks since I saw them last and Feather and I hadn't left off on the best note, but there were hugs all around. We sat down and had a breakfast of eggs, bacon, and Skip's specialty: one holers (a piece of toast with a hole in the middle an egg is cooked in. When you cut into the bread the yolk gets everywhere and the bread soaks it up, they're 10/10).

"So, last I heard you were being a bit too creative for your own good," Feather joked.

"Shit man, it was pretty nuts. I think I'm done with that, for now at least," I replied.

"Good man, but look, we've got shit to do. The label assholes want us to do another album, but they fucked us man. Some lawyer Drew hired came to Laura and I after he bailed and told us about how shitty this contract is. I'd assumed we got fucked off the bat, but I didn't know it was that bad," Feather said.

"Take a look at this, it's what I've been doing since I got down here," I said as I handed Feather the notebook containing all the songs I wrote. "I've been a bit busy if you couldn't tell, and I also think I figured out a way around this contract BS. Euphoric Blue is tied up, Euphoric Blue can't make any music unless it's through Steinberg and his assholes, but The Bums, The Bums are free of any contract. Skip's girlfriend knows a guy with some recording equipment that's better than what we had in San Francisco, but obviously it's not as good as the shit in the study in LA. That being said, I say we give it a shot and get working ASAP. Drew's in, are you guys?" I explained.

"I'm down. Thank god for you and your dumbass," Feather said.

"I have one condition: we surf before we record everyday. Feather and I have our instruments in the TTM. We brought your drum set down too, Drew. We surf after breakfast, then we get to work," Laura said, a strong hint of authority in her voice.

It was the first time we had all been out in the water together in a really long time. The waves weren't big at all, and we were all on longboards. Feather said he hand't rode one since he learned to surf, so I spent thirty minutes on the beach showing Feather how to dance. It was the first time I'd really talked to him since the night of my trip. He explained the whole punk thing in detail and in reality, he was just trying to impress a girl and get us off the label. But, he decided to stop chasing said girl when he realized he was changing himself for somebody else. Thankfully for him, this girl Stacy decided to start chasing him back, and it sounded like Skip wasn't the only one who decided to tie themselves down.

We paddled out together and rode the first three waves together. Feather being on that wave next to me was like having my own brother back. He would never admit it, but I think he felt the same way. He got his first nose ride, and he was ecstatic. Ethan paddled back to the lineup and there was a look of childlike wonder in his eyes. Unlike when I left LA, Feather was relaxed, happy, and chilled out.

We paddled back in and each of us was starving and ready for food. Skip had extra tacos and ceviche waiting for us back at the shop. Laura, Drew,

Feather, and I ate more then than I think we ever had before. We walked away with full stomachs and my notebook, and, within an hour, we were setting up our gear in a recording studio located in a garage.

Feather let me take the lead for the first time. I was the one singing but he still worked backup vocals. The sound to match my lyrics came out sounding like a mix between psychedelic rock, blues, and surf rock, and it had a style heavily resembling jazz. Every few songs, Feather would be the one to sing or we'd all start jamming and Feather would just sing whatever he was thinking and we'd take turns soloing our various instruments. Our longest jam went on for twenty minutes. Nobody knew who would throw in their bit next. It was spontaneous, fun, it was random. Hell, Feather ran out of words to say but singing a bunch of random sounds in a way that made up for him not having an instrument or lyrics. His voice was literally an instrument like no other.

Towards the end of the album, my voice was getting a bit hoarse and I wanted Ethan to take over, but Feather drove home that this was my album, my lyrics, and it had to be my voice. I couldn't do another song, so we started jamming again, but Feather wouldn't sing, so Erin's friend tossed Feather a harmonica and he went off on it. The last song went on for more than fifteen minutes, we sat and jammed and Feather wailed on the harmonica like nobody I'd heard before.

After we finished recording, we just sat and chilled in the garage. Erin's friend brought out a couple beers and put on headphones to get to work mixing songs and creating an album. By the end of the day we had recorded the whole album 3 different times. Bill, Erin's 40 and graying friend, was picking and choosing the best parts of each recording, mixing and matching, but doing what he could to keep the flow. The final jam was a single run and he was putting that one smack dab in the middle of the album. The other jams we did were to be released as singles throughout the week and they went completely untouched.

This was how it was meant to be, all of us together, in a garage, spending a whole day recording after a good surf, and then sitting back with a couple beers while the album got mixed. I thought this day couldn't get any better, hell I knew it couldn't. This was one of the best days of my life, but that's when it happened. It got better. She walked in, and it became the best day of my life.

"So you're the ones making all the noise! Funny to see you with clothes on for once," she said, the last statement directed at me.

"You can see them off again if you want," I responded to the girl with shoulder-length, blonde curls and gorgeous, blue eyes.

"You're Kevin right, the dumbass all over the news? Euphoric Blue, right?" she said, her voice filled with energy and pep.

"That would definitely be me, that's Ethan, but we call him by his last name, Feather. That's Drew over there, he plays drums, and that's our bassist Laura," I answered, nervously introducing each of my bandmates, and nervous was something I normally was not. "And who are you?"

"I'm Amy. What exactly are you guys doing here? I thought your band was on a label, why are you in this pigsty of a garage?" she said.

"Well, Euphoric Blue is on a label, and a label that fucked us. This is officially The Bums, an indie kinda thing," I said, she nodded and the following second of awkward silence lingered for eternity before I asked, "So, uh, is that like your dad or something?"

"Uncle. I'm from the New York, I'm headed back tonight, I'm starting rehearsals for a show tomorrow," she responded.

"Oh so you're an actress huh?" I said, semi-sarcastically

"I'm not an actor, I'm a performer bitch!" she said laughing this crazy laugh that just brought the whole room to life.

"Hey Kevin, we've gotta go so stop trying to get into Bill's niece's pants and let's head on out! Skip's barbecuing on the beach tonight, remember?" Drew said.

"Well I guess that's my cue. Tell your uncle thanks. What's your number? Maybe you could show me around the big city if I ever end up out there. I haven't been there since I moved when I was way younger," I asked while the lump in my throat was keeping me from breathing.

"Ya, I think I'd like that. Sounds like you've gotta go, though. I'll see you around hopefully," she finished, before taking my phone and quickly punching her number in.

"Oh Kevin, you asked for her number, that's something new! Does that mean you'll talk to her more than once?" Laura joked from shotgun.

"Ah fuck off! Like you're one to talk!" I said.

"Calm down you two, we're all whores here!" Feather said and we all laughed.

That night I was in a better mood than normal, and everything in general was better than normal. The fish filets and "Skip Taco Surprise" tasted better than any steak I had back in LA at the fancy restaurants I frequented and blew my signing bonus on. Skip played the same playlist he always played on beach barbecues, a mix of surf rock, Sublime, and Slightly Stoopid, and it all sounded brand new, despite the fact I knew every lyric to every song.

There was something about Amy that made everything ordinary, extraordinary and the extraordinary, otherworldly, and she wasn't even there. Our conversation was quick, short, and simple, but it didn't make a difference, I was beyond infatuated, beyond obsessed even. I felt something I couldn't begin to describe, nor wanted to attempt describing, as I knew doing so would do the feeling I felt an injustice.

So, I began to think of lyrics for a song. The only way I knew I could possibly describe an emotion was through the song, but it wouldn't be through the lyrics. When the time came to record said song I'd do a solo and use the instrument to invoke the feeling rather than use words to attempt describing it, as the feeling was beyond description in the same way the eternity I'd experienced through my drug-induced, ego deaths were. Shit, it was beyond the awe inspring event that is ego-death itself.

Whatever strange, pure thing was left behind when the ego was stripped away, that thing I saw in everything and everyone, that's what I felt. In all honesty, my attempt at describing the impossibility of a description of feeling such a feeling is doing an injustice beyond any other injustices seen by anybody in this life or any others, but even then I knew what that feeling was, you know what that feeling is, and we all know there's only one word that can describe it, but I won't use it now since I was too scared to use it then. Thankfully I can, in fact, use that word now and use it about three times a day no matter how many times Amy responds with the opposite. I know she means the same, but given my way of showing actual affection is through annoying her or by doing insanely over-the-top-romantic-thing-a-ma-jigs, she can't help but respond with I hate you. Sorry, spoilers! I couldn't help myself, but back to the story of that guy Feather, the whole reason you're reading this.

The night drew on and on, the bonfire we built was huge, and it was more magnificent than any that Skip made before that. Eventually all Skip's various beach bum friends who had turned out began turning in, Erin and Skip were the only ones who remained at the beach while Drew and I walked back up to the shop with Nacho. We spent our last night staying up late playing old video games on the tiny tv in the room we'd been sharing. Laura and Feather crashed in the van, and I knew they'd be up at around 5 for a surf. We sat in silence for hours and hours, simply just playing video games, before Drew finally admitted:

"You know I think I'm addicted to blow."

"Ya, I figured that out," I responded.

"But am I really addicted if it's not like, taking over you know?" he asked.

"Well, I mean ya, but you're not like a junkie I guess. Just don't become a junkie. Or overdose. I swear if you overdose and fuckin' die dude, I'm gonna fuckin' kill you."

"Thanks I think."

"Shit, is Skip banging again? Jesus, doesn't he realize we're awake?"

"I don't think he cares."

"Let's get to bed, we're headed east tomorrow."

Our first stop that morning was the lineup. The waves weren't anything to go nuts over, but they were waves nonetheless. Drew didn't even catch one, but shit, he still had a huge smile on his face. I'd come to the conclusion as long as he still made his own happiness, I wasn't gonna intervene, but the moment he got as bad as he was back in San Francisco or LA, I was gonna knock some sense into that dumbass.

I'd also come to the realization that only idiots do drugs, but they do them so other people don't have to. While psychedelics weren't physically the worst, mentally they did things that only an idiot would put themselves through, but there was still something to be learned from it, and a wise dumbass could take those lessons and teach them to the wise smartass, and that's why I think Feather did so many. He was definitely the wisest dumbass I knew, which is why he was the one coming up with all of our songs. That's also why most artists of any kind did or do drugs, otherwise they would just make a bunch of meaningless crap. Although, there's a few artists out there who are in fact, wise smartasses and simply learned from the wise dumbasses and their experiences through their art, like Wolfe, Kessey, Garcia, or even Feather at this point, and they formed their own message around that and went on to form their own art. But, most of those people realized that they didn't need to spread a message if they got it, since that's a lot of work and they knew that so they'd leave it up to the dumbasses while they sat back and chilled somewhere as some kind of bum until they died.

111

Bill and Skip were able to get our album onto iTunes (Bill was apparently busy the night before), and they both setup various social media pages. Feather had apparently been talking to various venues across the nation without telling any of us, and we had our first nationwide tour set up. It was to start in San Diego and work its way all the way to New York, which was perfect.

The last stop on the tour was exactly where I wanted to end up, and if all went as planned, by the time I was there I'd be truly rich and famous. Now, that's something I never wanted to be, but given that I actually had something to do now other than keep myself entertained until I bite the bullet, I realized I had to be since I for some reason decided to be a musician. For artists of any kind there's no middle ground. You make it or you don't, and one way you end up broke and playing at the subway for some subway, or you end up with a whole lot of money and the opportunity to actually have a family and a bed to sleep in. Either way, a true artist is happy, but in one scenario they get to share their happiness with people they're close to, and in the other they share it with random people they don't know. And, making random people happy is exactly what I was about to do. It was time for The Bums first tour.

PYRO

"Good evening you filthy fucks, we're The Bums and I hope you're all high enough for this. If not, I've got quite the present for you," Feather said before tossing dubs out to the crowd.

There were about three hundred and thirty three people packed into the tiny room that had a shitty bar in the back. Feather was drunk, Laura was high, Drew was tweaking, and I was almost as nervous as when I talked to Amy.

Feather kicked it off with one of our old songs he'd wrote back in San Francisco, which was surely a lawsuit of some kind since Euphoric Blue was signed to a bunch of pricks, but we played and played. The night raged on and the crowd got more and more into each song. Finally, we played one of my songs, I was the front man for a second there. Feather and I traded off on doing vocals, something we'd discussed doing beforehand. He didn't understand that although I was the hand, he had to be the mouth. Each time I opened mine the crowd loved it, but not as much as they loved him, never as much ad they loved him.

Feather's way with words was something entirely different, each person listened like their life depended on it before they lost their shit. We ended with a cover of "Whole Lotta Love" and Feather looked like a real rockstar singing and dancing. I felt like a real rockstar playing each chord like it was the last chord I'd ever play, then I realized, we were real rockstars.

We may be called The Bums, we all may have been bums, but we were fucking rockstars. I played my heart out that night, and everybody loved it. The song was over, but I didn't want the night to be, so I started soloing like I'd never soloed before. I utilized every bit of guitar playing knowledge I had and before I knew it, Feather was crowd surfing and shouting random shit into the microphone while my fingertips were bleeding. The calluses couldn't prevent them from getting torn up from the way I was playing, but there was no stopping it. I was fifteen minutes in before collapsing to my knees and playing a last few chords and laying on my back. The crowd cheered and screamed at the end of it all. The smell of smoke, cheap beer, and vomit filled the air. The people were there to party, and we gave them one.

We signed autographs and packed up our gear before hopping into our van. Feather got behind the wheel and fired up the TTM, and before we knew it we were at a new venue in Arizona, then one in Utah, and we were on our way to Denver before the Travelin' Trouble Machine finally broke down on the side of the road. We sat there, dumbfounded for about an hour, but our confusion was only out of why it took the old piece of junk to take that long to break down on the side of the road.

Each person partook in their substance of choice. There were about two thousand CDs that Billy had shipped us that were waiting in Denver, along with a bunch of people who had paid good money to see us. Overnight, The Bums became an underground sensation. Our Twitter page had over sixty five thousand followers within a week of its creation, and we had already sold more than forty thousand copies of our album on iTunes.

According to Skip, Steinberg was not pleased with our change of heart (and name), and the asshole was working on building a lawsuit. Thankfully, he had little to go on since we could do "covers" of Euphoric Blue's music and we were a different group at this point. Apparently though, somewhere in the contract we had agreed to making two albums with his recording company, so we did make another one while on the road. We recorded a bunch of fart noises on Feathers iPhone speaker and emailed it to him. We still had our full creative control.

"It's kinda like modern art. I'm almost sad we can't release it under The Bums," Feather said after shooting off the email.

"Well, now that problem is solved, what about the goddamn one where we're broken down in the middle of BFE and have to be in Denver in less than four hours?" Laura responded.

"Look, I'm sure we can figure out something! I mean, one of you knows how cars work, right?" Feather asked. We all shook our heads. "Shit."

"What about roadside assistance?" Drew questioned, and Laura instantly pulled out her phone to make a call.

"We've got to wait an hour and they'll be here. In the meantime, I'm gonna nap. Don't get yourselves killed," Laura said before retiring in.

We sat there for about ten minutes before Feather came up with the stupidest idea I'd ever heard.

"Highway golf. I've got a few clubs and a bunch of balls for it in the van. We go down that hill, line up, and if you make it across the freeway it's a point, hear a thunk, that's twenty five points, and if there's shouting following the thunk, that's another twenty five bonus points!"

"Feather that's the goddamn stupidest thing I've ever heard of," I said.

"So?" Drew added.

"So what? That's just asking for trouble!" I said.

"Kevin, you're a rockstar in a van called the Travelin' Trouble Machine. Your life is nothing but askin' for trouble. Unless you have any better ideas, we're playing some motherfuckin' highway golf," Feather finished.

Twenty minutes later we were down the hill with thirty golfballs each. Each of us had a different sized club, so things weren't too fair, but shit, it was fun. It took about ten shots before the first thunk, and another five before the first shout. Then we heard another thunk followed by a screech, WHABAM, and a lot of really loud shouting. A guy started coming down the hill, and none of us knew how many points we were to allot to the person who swung the club, nor did we really know which one of us hit the ball who hit the large, angry, bearded not-so-gentle man's car. I don't think he really cared. He saw us and our clubs, and started down the hill after us in a rage unlike any other I'd seen before. To make things all the more fun, behind him were two guys in leather jackets screaming about their bikes.

We booked it and made a mad dash for the treeline before we heard the loud crack of a gun being fired, and that's when the nitro kicked in. Drew,

116

Feather, and I barreled through the unexplored forest, snapping twigs, scaring off various little critters, and laughing like the mad men we were.   Distant profanities grew fainter before we all collapsed onto the ground, gasping for air and nearly suffocating from our laughter.   Cuts and scrapes riddled our exhausted bodies, and then Feather's phone started to ring.

Laura called and had seen the whole accident, nobody got seriously hurt, but one guy's car was royally fucked up. She didn't know what we'd been doing, but the moment she saw the guys running down the hill and yelling, she knew we were involved.

She texted Feather again when the coast was clear and we could head back up. The walk back took about another twenty minutes, and when we got back, I wish we hadn't. Laura was fucking livid.

"What in the hell were you guys thinking? I'd expect this from you two idiots, but you Kevin? Kevin, you're supposed be the one keeping them in check! You think I can make sure you idiots don't die all by myself? That guy had a gun, and he could've killed all three of you!   What do you guys have to say for yourselves?!?" Laura shouted.

"Sorry mom," I replied and the others burst into laughter.

"I swear to god... I'm touring America with a bunch of ten year olds! I'm not talking to any of you until we get to Denver! If you couldn't tell, I'm fucking pissed! I was taking a real good nap too!" Laura said.

The car was fixed within five minutes of the roadside assistance dude arriving, who arrived within five minutes of us getting our asses chewed out, and Laura wasn't lying when she said she wouldn't talk to us the rest of the car ride. Drew had decided to take

117

over driving while Feather and I sat in the back throwing various pieces of trash at Laura trying to get a reaction out of her. When that proved futile, we gave her a double wet willy, and all we got from that was a death stare that said more than another rage-fueled monologue could, so we both sat silently in the van for the remainder of the ride.

Denver was crazier than any of the venues before, since people actually knew who we were. Hell, the show was sold out! I got drunk as all hell before going on with Feather, something I hadn't done before. This wasn't regular drunk either, this was rockstar-drown-in-my-vomit drunk, and I immediately hated it

My playing was sloppier than normal, but my onstage antics were over the top. I danced from one end of the stage to the other, rolled around on the ground, and then promptly proceeded to puke on the front row of the crowd. To my disgust, they didn't seem to mind a bit that they were covered in vomit because it was my vomit. On our albums, our music was relaxed, stuff to chill out to, but live, we were an entirely different band. Feather had us do a couple of our songs from our punk album. Half the crowd was confused, but the other half started a mosh pit like none I'd seen before.

By the time we packed up, I could tell Feather troubled by something. Something was really off about him after the show.

"Kevin, I don't know if I want to tour if this is what touring is. It's fun, but shit man, I don't want to get drunk and sloppy and just play the same setlist every night for a bunch of people just trying to party. I miss the days in the apartment, shit man, I miss Baja,"

Feather said, his eyes watering.

"Dude, we don't have to play like this every night. Sure it's cool, but what we used to do and how we used to play is what's really us. That's what the people came out to see. Half that crowd hated what we were doin', and I think that was the half of our real fans," I said.

"What do we do then? People are gonna start expecting us to go nuts on stage," Feather said.

"We put more meaning in. We'll make up for the energy with passion. That's what we're missing. People love seeing others do what they're passionate about because it reminds them what they're passionate about. We're too focused on getting fucked up and putting on a good show that we're not really playing for ourselves, we're playing for money," I said.

"I like it. Maybe if we show our passion up here, it'll remind somebody down there of what they're passionate about and they'll pursue that instead of pursuing a paycheck and we'll save them from the cubicle. And, I guess as a bonus, that real half becomes the only people showing up to our shows, and I guess that's the only people we want showing up," Feather said while signing a CD for somebody who had just purchased one from Drew and Laura.

"Hey, can I get a picture?" the girl asked.

"Why not!" Feather responded. The girl handed me her phone and I took the picture of them for her.

"If it's worth anything, I think you're right. I like the music on your albums more, this didn't feel like The Bums, it just felt like another rock show," the girl said and she was off.

I could already tell by the look in his eyes that

Feather was taking each syllable of that sentence straight to his soul, and I knew that girl had saved the band.

We played twenty seven more shows before we got to New York for our final one, and, at this point, we were all over the internet. Within the months of our tour, we became a global sensation. We'd been working at it for more than two years, yet it felt like barely a day had passed. Yet, Christmas was a week away and it would be the third one I was to spend with Laura, Drew, and Feather, but our fame seemed overnight.

We went from a band that maybe thirty thousand people knew existed to an international sensation. Apparently The Bums self titled first album was at number 19 in Australia, 42 in the UK, and 21 on the US charts for alternative music. We had to book a different venue at the last few locations due to the drastic increase in demand for tickets, and the fact that New York was where (according to Spotify) we had the highest amount of listeners with two hundred thousand different people in NYC alone listening to our music every month.

Upon arriving, I sent Amy a picture of the city after not being in contact with her since I'd met her, and she called me the moment she read it.

"I was wondering when you guys would turn up! Looks like you're actually a rockstar now, but you're still a dumbass," she said.

"Why hello to you to! How've you been?" I asked.

We went on with boring small talk and I made all sorts of corny jokes that were only funny because they were the shittiest jokes anybody could think of. I told her I'd let her in backstage for our show, and I did. The entire time we played that night, I was on cloud nine. Every time I looked to my left and saw her smiling, I knew I'd found my dream girl. She was an artist in her own right, and Amy did things I don't think I ever could. I could barely lie, there was no way in hell I could act, and apparently she had managed to land a supporting role in a Broadway musical, something that I'd nearly shit myself just thinking about.

All in all, the show was like the others after Denver: magical, but even more so knowing I got to see Amy afterwards. After we packed our gear and sold our CDs, my other bandmates had left and it was just Amy and I sitting there.

"Alright, you told me you'd show me around the city, and I think you really should. I've only ever been where a sensible parent would take their ten year old. I want you to really show me the city. I wanna see what New York is really like," I told her.

"Well that's no problem at all, what do you want me to show you first?" she asked.

"Hm, how about a good place for dinner? My treat," I answered.

"Are you asking me out?"

"I definitely am."

"I might have a boyfriend."

"Well where is he?"

"I'm not sure, he's been getting a lot of texts from other girls, and," she broke down into tears at this point, "I just want to find somebody who's not a fucking asshole."

"Let me see your phone."

"Why?"

"Just let me see your phone."

"What the hell did you just do?"

"Well, I took care of the asshole problem, sounds like you've dealt with too many of those. How about you give a dumbass a try."

"Jesus, Kevin. Fine, ya, let's go get dinner," Amy finished, giving me a big hug, her eyes lighting up like they did the first time I met her. "You know you're a cheesy motherfucker, right?"

"Oh of course, it's my speciality," I responded with a smile before we both chuckled and headed out.

We went to a really classy place with menu items that costed as much as I used to spend in a week on food, but it was well worth the price. The restaurant was on the third story of a building downtown with quite the view. The waiter recognized me and didn't have a problem with skipping on the whole ID thing when I ordered a bottle of wine (I was only three weeks away from my 21st anyway). You know, I'm no expert on livestock, but I'm pretty sure the steak I was convinced to order costed more than an actual cow did.

"I think I could buy a lifetime supply of tacos with the money I just dropped on this steak," I joked on the meals arrival.

"Take a bite," she said. I did and I realized that every penny was worth that single bite. The steak tasted like nothing I'd ever had before.

"Holy shit, that's a kickass steak," I responded.

"Right?" she asked, and then I started playing with it. "I think you might secretly be a child in a twenty year old's body."

"Secretly?" I said.

"Okay you're a child in a twenty year old's

body. So, how did you even get that band together?" she asked.

I told her my story with the band and Feather (at least the story so far). She was intrigued the whole time, and I realized how insane it all was while I told her. I didn't even believe any of it was real life. My life. This wasn't just some fantasy, this was real. I even told her about the incident before Denver when Drew, Feather, and I nearly got shot and the time back in Baja when I nearly got eaten by a shark.

"So you're telling me in the past two or so years, you formed a band because you and a couple people you met on acid at a concert did acid in Mexico, played at some random venue, almost got murdered by a shark, and then almost got shot by some biker hick before becoming like the biggest newcomers to the scene? That's all so random, it's unbelievable! I literally would've died from a panic attack at least 60 thousand times in the first week. I'm kind of a safety freak. I can't force myself to take a risk like that! You're a special kind of dumbass, Kevin," Amy laughed.

"Well, I mean I think that's a compliment so thank you, I'm gonna take it as one," I joked, "but really, I just decided I'd live. All these random opportunities came up, and I took them. What's the point of living if you're not gonna take all the things life throws your way?"

"Well you can't live if you die!" she said, the tone of the conversation took a somewhat serious one.

"I'd rather die with a smile on my face than live bored out of my mind. Shit, if I hadn't dropped with Feather or talked him into meeting me in Baja, we wouldn't be here right now. I'd probably be working the register at Skip's shop," I said.

"I guess you're right, but what about all the little things you could enjoy if you lived a normal life? You know the kind of life where you don't almost die or take an excessive amount of drugs every few weeks?" she asked.

"Well then I'd enjoy the small moments, but I'd be bored when I'm not."

"Are you trying to say that you don't get bored?"

"Well, I mean I do get bored, but like, it only lasts the amount of time it takes me to get from wherever I'm sitting around bored to a guitar."

"Here's your check," the waiter interrupted. I didn't even want to look at the check, so I just took five hundred dollars out of my wallet and handed it to him, told him to keep the change.

"You don't really live up to your band name. I don't know a single bum who carries that much cash," Amy said while we walked out into the gorgeous, lit up downtown.

"Well, if it makes you feel any better I'm technically homeless unless you count the back room at Skip's shop, or our rickety, rusty, ratchet-ass old band van, which we've named the Travelin Trouble Machine," I said.

"Oh wow, you're really trying to impress me on the first date, huh?" she said.

"You know it," I said before she stopped and grabbed my hand. Christmas lights had just been hung up downtown and Amy looked happier than a kid in a candy store.

"I fucking LOVE CHRISTMAS!" she exclaimed. "We have to go to the Rockefeller center!"

So, the night took us to the Rockefeller Christmas tree, which I remember going to when I was really little. It was the last place I remember being with my whole family, even my cousins were there who I completely lost touch with after one of them passed away promptly after his dad went out. Looking back on it, death kind of ran in the family.

"What is it Kevin?" Amy asked.

"Don't worry about it," I said and smiled. "Where do you think they grow a tree like this, because that's a big fuckin tree? Imagine if this whole tree was, well tree."

"I think I actually hate you," she chuckled.

"I know, but that's okay, I'm the best worst person you'll ever meet," I said before wrapping my hands around her waist.

I felt her arms around my neck before I leaned in and kissed her, and she kissed me. All I could think was, how lucky could one guy be? I mean shit, I did have really good luck with everything that had led up to that moment. Maybe it was the universe trying to make up for a shitty start... and that's when I heard somebody shout her name and realized: nobody is that lucky.

A tall, muscular guy approached, and he looked more pissed off than I think the bikers and the bearded guy were back in Colorado, but there was no forest to run into here. He had about three inches of height on me and at least forty pounds. On top of that, he probably did a lot more fighting than my hippy ass. Hell, I hadn't been in a fight since I tackled a kid through a table three years ago at the last party Drew and I went to before our road trip.

"Is there a problem, man?" I asked.

"Ya there fuckin' is! You're kissin' my fuckin' girl!" he said.

"Ah, so you're her recent ex. Maybe if you weren't ya know, a cheating asshole, we wouldn't be in the current situation," I replied.

"Kevin don't you don't ha-" Amy tried to say.

"Oh now I know where I recognize you from. I saw you play tonight, it's a shame. You've got some talent, but it's too bad I'm gonna have to break your skinny fingers!" the guy said before he shoved me back.

I knew that the guy was just trying to build up his confidence and break down mine, so I didn't give him a chance to do anything more. I fired off two jabs and a cross as quickly as I could before eating a big right hand, and then taking a wild swing to my gut, which knocked the wind out of me. I crumpled and he was on top of me, wailing on my ribs that were already bruised from an alcohol related fall a few nights before. The relentless rain of blows seemed like they wouldn't stop, so I grabbed my adversary's ankle and rolled towards it, bringing him to the ground, and now, I was in control. I got up and started kicking him in the side before somebody came running from the side and sucker punched me right in the sweet spot. I fell to the ground and smashed the left side of my head against the concrete before being enveloped by darkness.

When I regained consciousness somebody was standing above the guy who sucker punched me (now with a bloody nose and on the ground), yelling at him for "being a dishonorable coward". Amy was next to me, speechless. A large crowd surrounded us and I saw people taking pictures with their phones. The flash going off made me feel like vomiting, so I did. People were shuffling around due to what I assume were police officers coming to break up the fight. Amy's ex was still on the ground, holding his sides and coughing up a good amount of blood.

"Oh my god, Kevin, I'm so sorry. You really didn't have to do that, I'm so sorry," she said, sniffling. "This is all my fault, are you okay? I'll take you to a hospital."

"No, it's fine we could've just walked away, it's on me. I'm fine, we don't need to go to a hospital," I replied.

"You just hit your head against the concrete and puked! We're going to the hospital right now!" she said, but right when she helped me up, the two officers came up and began questioning us.

Amy and I told the officers what happened, and they let us go. Her ex and his friend got booked for assault and battery, thank god they were fans. Hell, one they gave us a ride to the hospital, where we found that I did, in fact, have a concussion, and a serious one at that.

I wasn't allowed to think too hard (thank god I already didn't) for the next few weeks, but that meant I wasn't allowed to play any music or do shows. I was outraged until I realized that the doctors weren't following me home.

Amy was about to leave before she asked, "Kevin, do you even have a place to stay?"

"I was just gonna crash in the van with the other three," I answered.

"You just got a concussion! Come back to my place, and you can spend the night there. You definitely shouldn't be sleeping in a van," she commanded, so I followed her to a cab. I was definitely not going to argue with the girl who looked like Marilyn Monroe (but better) when she told me to go back to her place.

Amy's apartment was across the water in the southernmost part of Brooklyn. The area she lived in was a bit on the rougher end, but not to the point where it made me feel uneasy. I'd spent plenty of time back in LA in much worst areas. It was a decently sized one bedroom apartment with a nice kitchen and a small living room adjacent to it. We went straight into her room so I could lay down, my head had been spinning the whole time, but I never gave her reason to suspect I was less than fine. We laid down and turned on some music since I wasn't supposed to watch TV, although after about twenty minutes of annoying her I convinced her to switch to MTV, who was broadcasting Jackass 2. Albeit a masterpiece, Amy's reactions to the stunts and stupidity were honestly funnier than the movie itself.

"You're telling me you actually like this?" she said.

"Well hell ya I do! What's there not to like? It has big stunts, dick jokes, and is honestly pure art!" I said.

"Are you trying to say that a guy sticking a fish hook in his mouth and jumping in shark infested waters is art? Or that guy drinking horse cum actually means something?"

"Well, ya. I don't think they were out there trying to spread some grand message, but I think Jackass does have an accidental message: live until you die. All those guys just don't give a fuck and do what they want. They're living life and making the most out

128

of it.   Even with everybody telling them they're dumbasses, dolts, and degenerates, they just do whatever they like because it's funny and they have fun. Like that scene where Dunn brands Bam, and then they go to Bam's mom.   Bam's mom kept asking Dunn 'why?' over and over again until there was only a single answer to the question remaining: it was funny. They're not doing it so much for the money, or for girls because I don't know about you, but if I were a girl I wouldn't be drooling over the guy who takes nut shots for a living- imagine how deformed that shlong is! They're just doing it because it's funny.   It brings them some kind of joy I'd assume.   I mean sure, they probably go a lot harder now that they can make millions off of their stunts, but what's the point of living if you're not going to enjoy living?" I rambled.

"I think you're the only person in the world who could see the 'art' behind Jackass," she said.

"Everything is art!   I mean we exist purely to exist and enjoy existence, and that's what art ultimately is.   Either the creator of the piece of art enjoys making it, or an artist finds happiness from seeing other people enjoy that art.   Ultimately, nothing matters, at all, so why not just have a good fuckin' time?   That's what I found out that night I ended up naked in the sand."

"How exactly did you end up like that anyway?"

"Shrooms.   I took a bit more than I should've that night, and well, I ended up in San Diego in Skip's shop.   I don't really remember what happened there, I was tripping way too hard.   I don't even remember the police picking me up, but I think when they came I was fast asleep from not sleeping all night."

"Why in the world would you take shrooms or

129

acid or any of that? Doesn't that shit make you go crazy or something?"

"Only the fake stuff, that's really the only danger; buying fake acid or not having a tripsitter when you're taking a dose you're not used to. I've tripped probably thirty times on acid, and ballpark twenty on shrooms. I'm a somewhat functional human being, I think. I get this thing called HPPD that acts up if I'm way too high where there'll be tracers and weird visual stuff, but, since that trip, I don't really like smoking anymore."

"But, still, why would you put yourself through that? It doesn't sound fun at all!"

"It's not about fun, it's about what you can learn from it. It takes you to some dark places and some amazing ones, but it's not what you experience it's what you get out of that experience. I honestly wouldn't have realized that music is my passion without it, and I wouldn't have quit abusing weed and would've quit the band without it. But, that being said, I don't need it anymore. Do drugs until you don't need to anymore, and I don't, so I'm not gonna, except for maybe weed sometimes. Like if I'm gonna surf and it feels like I should, I might have an extremely small amount, or maybe if I ever enter an eating contest, because let me tell you somethin about how much I can eat when I've got the munchies..."

We talked the night away until we were both exhausted, and I realized my knack for storytelling then and there with her, and the fun I found from it. A couple ideas started to pop into my head for songs, but I pushed them to the back of my mind to focus on the gorgeous girl curled up next to me. I told her goodnight and kissed.

Almost any given night I found myself curled up next to a girl (which was a good eighth of them) it was because I just fucked them or I was about to, but Amy, I didn't want to fuck her. I mean eventually I wanted to have sex, but I didn't want to fuck her. I wanted so much more than that, and I could already tell I'd gotten myself into what Skip classified as the worst kind of trouble in creation (although he did have a girlfriend himself). That trouble was an actual relationship.

My mind raced, and it hurt my head to think, but I decided Amy was more than worth a thought and sat there debating whether or not I'd actually let myself get tied down. Brian and my ego argued until Brian eventually convinced my ego that it was time to stop going for a body count and actually be happy, so I decided to be happy. I squeezed Amy a bit tighter, and then I let myself fall asleep.

BAD MOON RISING

A year, an album, and a series of presidential fuck ups had passed. Amy was headlining Broadway shows, Drew started doing television, Laura was a model, and Feather was somewhere in Nepal. Our first tour date for the "Bummin' It" tour was in four days, and I was sitting in mine and Amy's Manhattan penthouse in a mad panic. I hadn't talked to Feather since he left four months ago, and I was starting to get worried he'd lose track of time during his not-so-little spiritual journey.

"Bonfire Stories", our second album, was at number 2 on the US charts and top 20 in nearly every country where rock 'n' roll was still somewhat popular. I'd released a few singles talking about how stupid politics and those involved were. Some of them during the off-year election talking about the blatant corruption, and a final one after which was a soft-rock melody by the name of, "We're Fucked". Donald Trump was our president, extreme conservatives held control of all three government bodies (so much for checks and balances), and my pop tarts were burning.

Amy was out at rehearsals, so I dropped by and brought her lunch before giving Drew and Laura calls to express my excitement to hit the road with them. Drew had upgraded the speakers on the TTM, fixed the engine to avoid another incident like the one we had during our first tour, and partied harder than ever according to TMZ.

Due to a conflict in schedule, Amy wasn't due to join us on our tour until we got into the south, which was an increasingly terrifying place to be. Race riots ran rampant, political rallies held down there looked like the videos I remember Skip showing me of Hitler's rallies (and I'm not just talking about the crazy crowds, apparently the alt-right liked the Roman salute as much as the Nazis did), and with global temperatures increasing, that meant humidity in America's armpit was too.

I'd spent the past few months after the album doing nothing more than cute couple things with Amy. We had a shitzu named Coco that was little more than a glorified stuffed animal. Personally I was hoping for a wolf-dog, but apparently Amy didn't feel comfortable owning an animal that was illegal to have, and the same size of me. To make up for it, she finally let me get a snake. For our one year anniversary I took her to Disneyland, which was the one thing she loved more than Christmas, but given that it was Christmas while we were in Disneyland she basically burst into tears from happiness every twenty minutes.

I was taking my usual afternoon walk in Central Park after grabbing my meatball sandwich from the deli nearby. I went to the same place every time since the owner wasn't big into "the Devil's Music", and he simply knew me as Kevin. Since I had to walk around with a hat and sunglasses everywhere I went, I kind of realized that fame sucked ass. It let me do what I wanted with my life, but the combination of my music's popularity, early career antics, and the fact I didn't hold back in voicing my opinions, made me a media favorite. A few paparazzi punching incidents later, and I realized the best way to go about things was to just ignore the assholes and they'd eventually learn to ignore me.

Feather had quite the year, to say the least. He locked himself in his humble home in LA for three days straight on a giant ayahuasca binge before coming back with three different book series taking place in a place called Oreia. In addition, he had a notebook filled with lyrics. None of them made sense at first, until I realized that he'd written each song out across a line in the notebook. He didn't write a line and move down to the line below it, no, he wrote the next line on the adjacent page. It took us days to actually write out the lyrics in a way that made some form of sense, and then we pounded out our new album in about three weeks in the high-end recording studio Billy built.

After the album was released, he began touring America with shows where he'd just sit with an acoustic guitar, and he'd just sit and play music. Feather would sing whatever popped into his head, and then he'd talk for thirty minutes at a time. Feather did what I never thought he would as he expressed no interest in the topic, but he talked politics and voiced his strong opposition against the direction the country headed towards. He'd rant and ramble the first words that came to his head and people paid to hear him do so. Thousands of people paid to hear him do so. They'd sit and they'd listen and he'd stand and inspire.

He spent another few months protesting an oil pipeline being built in North Dakota, and he would play his guitar while unarmed people marched towards police officers and private security spraying pepper spray, throwing tear gas, shooting rubber bullets, and they even released attack dogs on the self-titled water-protectors. He released a few singles that talked about the horrors he witnessed while people were "fighting" to protect their sacred lands and basic necessity: water. This really riled up a good portion of our fan base and pissed off a good amount of powerful assholes. The media couldn't enough of him, and he fuckin' hated it. So, he did what any sensible human being does at some point in their life, and Ethan disappeared to Nepal on some spiritual quest.

Out of everybody I'd say I was the most low-key. Snowboarding when I could (I hated the frigid waters of New York, so I picked it up not too long after buying a place), but I mostly just hung out and chilled with Amy and Coco. I only really spoke up like Feather did when he disappeared, and I went on a few popular podcasts and radio shows before starting my own to rant and ramble randomness and my opinions.

The most notable night of all was when I was visiting some friends back in San Francisco and went to a bar up in Marin where none other than Bobby Weir was playing, so I went up and jammed with him. To my surprise, he recognized me as Kevin the rockstar and shook my hand and everything until I reminded him it wasn't the first time we met. He wasn't the least bit surprised that I went on to do what I did and after a couple drinks together, we parted ways again but he promised me it wouldn't be the last time I saw him.

It was on my bench in Central Park when he called me, "Your buddy Feather is at my house. I'm not sure how he got in, but he says meet at the old studio apartment when it's time to tour again."

"Bob, is that you?"

"Ya, I don't know how he found his way here, but he's a cool guy."

135

"Right? Well I guess I'll see him then."

"Oh ya, I'll see you around Kevin!"

"Wait!"

"Ya?"

"Would you mind opening for us on our first night of the tour? It would be an honor like no other, man."

"Sure, why not! I guess I'll see you there too, but I've got to go. Bye now."

"Bye Bob."

Holy shit, did Bob Weir just call me? This can't be real life. I'll pinch myself. Ow, ya this is real oh my god Bob Weir is opening for MY band. Goddamn...

Four days later I was sitting outside the old apartment with my guitar case, a small duffel bag filled with clothes, and my board bag containing my favorite shortboard and the longboard I'd shaped with Skip last time I visited. The show was at Shoreline, which I thought was very appropriate since it was where I first truly grabbed a guitar. It was amazing, the crowd was shocked when Bob came out and opened and I swear somebody spiked my water bottle with acid because he stayed on stage and played guitar with me!

Given the circumstances we started with a cover of Truckin, which really made a lot of sense to play. It really had been a long, strange trip to the point in my life I was in. Standing up there and playing in front of tens of thousands made me really reflect, and I realized again that I owed this moment to taking random opportunities that had to defy insane odds to present themselves. All I had I owed to chance.

We ended with another cover, Ripple, my

favorite dead song. Bob, Feather, and I all sang it together, and, after we sang the last lyric, I hugged both of them. I was overcome with emotion, and I rushed backstage where none but Amy was waiting to surprise me. I gave her a big hug and couldn't contain my overwhelming happiness. Originally she wasn't going to be able to make it out for the first show of the tour, but I guess she found a way to get out of a rehearsal for a show she was a lead in, and she came all the way out to see me.

She'd really made her way in Broadway. Within a year of meeting her, Amy went from occasionally getting a decent role as ensemble or as a supporting character after countless auditions, to being asked to play leads. That was partly due to some short films we made with friends that I wrote specifically to showcase her amazing acting skills. Hell, she'd even won a Tony, but that didn't change the fact she was the last person I expected to be backstage after that concert, and the only one I truly wanted to see there.

I didn't know what to do I was happier than I'd ever been so I cried, and I never cried, ever, but that moment was honestly the best way to end the best night of my life. Everybody came backstage and we had a big group hug, after which Drew reminded me to: "Grow a pair of balls and quit crying, if it's gonna be like this every night, I think I might end up driving my drum sticks through my eyes! Now who's ready to go out?"

That's when Bob parted ways with the band and I. We went to a bar and I only had a single beer while everybody else drank a bit too much. The night ended with all of us, even Amy, in the van, and shit, the van looked amazing. It still looked like the rickety old bum van it was, but the inside had two futons and a roof that popped up with enough space for two to share a bed. Amy and I slept up top and peered through the clear-plastic roof at the stars. We pondered life, the universe, and everything.

"What are the odds that all of this happens? I could've just got that guitar from Bob Weir that night years ago, and it all could've ended there. I would've been fine, but all of this has just, like, happened you know? I still can't accept that any of this is even real. This can't be real. It's too amazing. You're too amazing," I whispered to Amy with a smile.

"Well, if there's a one in a million chance of something happening, it has to happen to somebody," she said.

"I guess. I'm exhausted babe, I think I'm gonna go to sleep. Night my princess," I said and kissed her.

"You deserve some sleep, you've had a big fuckin' day! Goodnight, sleep well cutie," she said and kissed me back.

Early that morning I woke up Drew, and I had him drive us to the airport so Amy could catch her flight home. We went on and continued our tour, taking a different route than last time. We went up north, hit New York where we took a momentary break, and I got to show my friends around the city I'd fallen in love with. Then we caught a plane and flew to the UK. We were a sensation over there!

First up was London, which was insane! The people there were really in love with rock music. It was a huge culture shock since America's music taste was as diverse as its people. We'd spent our time before our show there sight seeing and going to various important spots in music history. That night we played on the same stage the Beatles once performed on, and it was one the most humbling experience of my entire life.

Next, we hit Edinburgh, and then it was back down to Bristol, after which we went and spent some time in Canterbury, where Feather and I went around and played guitar at random street corners for no real reason. We went to Cardiff where we played a sold out show and caught a train north to Glasgow to play another amazing show. After that I visited the Morton castle (I was a quarter Scottish on my dad's side and it was because of those guys) with Feather.

I sat outside it playing guitar, and Feather made up sang ballads and stories of great warriors. Whether any of the stories he was telling were true, I would never know, but while we did that I thought of all the random crazy events that led up to the building of that castle hundreds of years ago. Then, I began to think about the random crazy events that led to my birth and so and so forth. I sat and played in a trance fueled by nothing other than amazement at how crazy everything was that led to that very moment, and then I started wondering if anybody else had wondered the same thing in that spot.

"I'm sorry Kevin," Feather said.

"For what, man?"

"Remember the night we got into a fight before you went on that shroom trip?"

"Ya, what about it?"

"You guys are my family. I said we weren't. I said we never were, but I didn't mean it. I don't know if you know this, but I didn't exactly have the best home life. My parents were junkies. My brother raised my sister and I until my sister died and my brother shot himself. My parents didn't give a shit. They were just bummed they weren't gonna get the same money from the state they were getting before, so I left. That's when I met Lauralyn, I was homeless, and she used to bring me food everyday. We became friends and she introduced me to real music, and I introduced her to weed. Two years later, we went to a dead concert and I guess you can figure out the rest.."

"Shit Ethan, I didn't know that."

"Ya, that's when I started writing too. You know I wrote stories before I wrote songs? I guess it was just how I escaped. When I created my own world, shitty things couldn't happen to me if I was in control, you know? I could be whoever I wanted. I could be a pirate, a viking, a Celtic warrior, I always liked writing fantasy stories and those kinds of things. Everything was about honor and it was so easy to write about a brave warrior who was strong and kind and honorable, everything I wasn't. I've done some shitty things, Kevin. I haven't always been the kind of guy you think I am. I'll tell you some of those stories sometime after the tour, but I've got plans for when this is all finished we have to see through first."

"Whatever you were isn't what you are now, man. I lost my brother and dad when I was young too. Skip was all I had 'til Drew came along. You're not alone anymore, your family is huge now, and it's not just me and Laura and Drew anymore. It's all of our fans, it's Amy, it's Skip too, it's everybody. Your family is everybody you've touched, Ethan, and you've reached a lot of fuckin' people. Now let's get going, we're playing Dublin tomorrow night, and then we're headed back to New York to get the van. Then it's to

140

Atlanta, so we have a lot of pubs to get to before we go back stateside. The drinking culture here makes me actually want to drink!"

In the few weeks we were away and isolated from the domestic problems of our home country, racial tensions had escalated as well as international tensions. Middle eastern countries and terrorist groups had banded together to create a true Islamic State that consisted of the lands that were once known as Iraq, Iran, Afghanistan, Egypt, Jordan, Libya and Syria. Israel was in the middle of a nasty invasion, and it was bound to fall within the month. The weapons they had were rumored to be those of mass destruction, and they were made out as the greatest threat to western society since Buddhism.

I hadn't been exposed to the culture of the deep south before, but, when we got to Georgia, it was obvious what they wanted and it was blood. Churches, that were supposed spread the message of peace and love had signs on their lawns advertising war and bigotry. In Atlanta there were people on street corners preaching hate to the passerby, and I even witnessed the beatdown of a gay guy. I knew that it wasn't like this before, but, ever since the power had shifted, the attitude of the nation, the attitude of the people followed.

Society was taking steps back in places like the south. A divide in the very country was being created that hand't been seen since the nineteenth century (ideals from then were remerging as well), and it looked like we were on the brink of a second Vietnam, but when I looked at Feather, all he cared about was getting to the show.

We arrived at our venue to crowds of people who strongly disagreed with the things Feather had been saying on his brief solo tour. People waited outside to spit on us while they screamed various profanities. We made a mad dash for the stage. Atlanta was a big city too, and those were traditionally more progressive and rational, so I was not looking forward to the rest of the tour.

By the time we got to one of our last locations in Alabama, people were going nuts. Trash was getting thrown by white trash. I remember on my way up to the show, a bottle hit me in the head and I stumbled and saw stars, but after regaining my footing I kept walking towards the venue with the other three, who weren't phased by the abuse. Somebody reached across the barrier and grabbed Laura's chest, and then Feather did the most un-Feather thing I could think of.

Ethan reached over the barrier, grabbed the guy, then he proceeded to punch the hell out of him. Blood streamed down the redneck's face and decorated Feather's knuckles until Drew and I had to pull him off. There was outrage by the group of around 50 and they nearly broke down the barrier before police officers started spraying pepper spray on the crowd, and we ran into the backstage before locked the door behind us, and muting what was close to a riot just outside.

Despite what had happened, we proceeded to play our concert to the war-hawks' disdain, but their opinions didn't really hold any sway over any of us. After our last song people started to file out, satisfied with the show, but not thrilled. Then Feather grabbed the microphone.

"Wait! I urge you all to listen to what I have to

say," he shouted into the device, most stopped and turned. "We live in troubled times. Tensions run high throughout the nation and throughout all of us. I'd like to apologize to the man I beat outside. That was uncalled for. Sir, if you see this or hear about this, I want you to know I will pay any medical bills or cover any other inconvenience that has arose from my actions. I want to remind you all that violence is never the answer. There is always another way. Everybody, Christian, Muslim, Republican, Democrat, black, white or whatever religion, creed, or group each person identifies with, wants peace. The message behind every religion, the end result of each holy book is peace, love, and unity. That's what we aim to achieve, but we cannot do that ourselves. A month from now I will return to Standing Rock with my bandmates. Our planet is not a renewable resource, and we are the ones who have to protect it. But, this goes beyond simply protecting a water source. It's about standing up to people who are bullies, taking what they want from innocent, defenseless people, and threatening their very ways of life. What I'm trying to say, is I want you all to not only stand with us and Standing Rock, but I want you to stand with the world. I want you all to stand with us for peace and for love, for unity and for true justice. We are a nation on the brink of a war that will end like Vietnam did, but worst. If bullets are used before words, our biggest export will become young men and women, and our biggest import will be bodybags. People will die to fight a threat that was created by us and our greed," Feather began to say before being interrupted.

"Get the hell off stage!" a man shouted from the back.

"Sir, I apologize if he's saying things you don't agree with. If it bugs you, you can leave and carry on living your life. Have a good night," Laura butted in.

"Thank you Laura. So, when President Trump asks you to fight in his 'war on terror', I want you to realize it's a war for money coming at the expense of the most precious thing this universe has to offer, and that thing is life! Stand with us, stand with peace, and stand with this planet. When hatred looks you in the face and spits on you, do not do as I did and spit back. Instead, keep your chin up and give hatred a hug. If we fight fire with fire, the inferno will only grow. Love is the water to put this fire out, and it's up to all of you, up to all of us, up to everybody, to be the ones to provide that water. Even if it's something small, it makes a difference. Thank you all, you were a great crowd. Goodnight," and then Feather walked off. Laura, Drew and I remained, and, after another few minutes of silence, it was just the crowd and I.

Something told me to stay on stage, I should've gone backstage, gone back to my hotel room and watched a movie with Amy, but I stayed and then I saw it. Feather left the acoustic I got him on stage so I took my guitar off and I grabbed his. I thought of my dad's favorite artist, Johnny Cash, and I played "I Won't Back Down". I played it much slower than I'd ever heard it before. The people who had began to leave stopped in their tracks and turned to listen and watch. A group of people in the front began to sing with me and eventually the whole crowd joined in by the end of the song. Afterwards everybody cheered and I put the guitar down and just sat there and watched everybody file out. A couple lingered and I could tell they were contemplating asking me for autographs or something of the like, but they realized now was not the time. When the huge venue was empty and the thousands of people had finally left, I sat there alone and I cried.

IMAGINE

We returned to LA after cancelling the rest of the tour due to safety concerns. Feather immediately got to work. I bought a small, beach front house that Amy and I were living in for the time being. She wasn't going to be in another show for a few months, and we were finally able to simply be together again.

I taught her to surf. She was scared of the ocean but she was a natural, and after the first time she stood up, that fear melted away. She was afraid of nothing and realized that. As JFK once said, "the only thing we have to fear is fear itself," and those words ring true in every facet of life. Nearly anything and everything bad that happened, happened out of fear. Militaries were built in fear of people attacking, but those people are only attacking because they're scared of being hit first, so they strike back first (if that makes sense). In a relationship, if one person is terrified of hurting the other person or being hurt, that causes them to hold back and eventually, their fear comes true but it is because of that terror that the prophecy is fulfilled. Trust me on this, the moment you realize fear is fake and feeds off itself, it won't bug you anymore.

One morning we were on the beach, when Feather approached us with the strangest of company: Tom Morello and Paul McCartney.

"We're doing an album before Standing Rock," Feather said, Paul and Tom were behind him and talking amongst themselves.

146

"What? We're leaving in a week and a half! We can't make and record an album!" I said.

"I got in contact with every artist I could, it's not just us, it's a bunch of us. We thirteen different people from street performers to those two. The name of the group is the Ambassadors. The album is going to be mostly covers. Each group or individual is doing a song of their choice, cover or their own, and finally we're going to do one song that everybody is going to play on," Feather explained.

"Doesn't really sound like you're asking, when do we start recording?" I said.

"In about an hour and a half," he said.

"What?!?" I exclaimed.

"We have to do this, Kevin. I know you wanted some downtime before Standing Rock, but this album has the potential to change a lot, and there's already too much I've already set in motion and committed to. They're all coming with us to Standing Rock. We're doing a show there. Be at Bill's studio by one thirty," Feather finished before walking off and getting in a car with the two superstars.

"He's not normally like that, is he? That's a lot and he kind of just dropped it on you," Amy said.

"No, but he's got a vision and when he's got a vision he makes it happen. Fuck, I just wanted to chill. Oh well, let's go get lunch and then you can come to the studio to watch us record," I said and we left for our favorite taco shop.

I sat in the room filled with people I idolized and realized that I wasn't just meeting them, I was working with them. An obscure Jamaican artist named Brushy One String was there, he was the most interesting of all. He played amazing music with a guitar that only had one string, and he was jamming with Rome when we walked in. The two of them entered the studio and played "Zimbabwe" and "The Sound of Silence" (for which Bushy used a six string for once).

Next up was us, The Bums, and Feather told us to play "Come Together". A Boston band, Dispatch, was there, and they played their own song "The General". When they came back in, I told them that song was the first I ever played, so they decided to rerecord it with my guitar accompanying them. A truly surreal experience. Then, Robert Plant and Keith Richards (with the help of Drew and Laura) played "Going to California" and "Sympathy for the Devil". When my band mates came out of the room they had a look beyond disbelief on their face.

We were the biggest band on the scene at the moment, but these guys were all beyond us. This was a room filled with many of the most talented, influential musicians of the past 50 years. The most insane part? They were all there because Ethan asked them to be.

Even when the day of recording was done, the fun wasn't. We all sat around and talked and jammed for a few hours. It was the most fun I'd ever had, we were doing what music was meant to do: make change and, more importantly, having fun.

Amy didn't recognize a good half of the superstars there, but when I started explaining exactly who was who while we were walking to the car, she was in shock. I really thought that this would do something, seeing all these artists banding together to do something more than just make music for fun, even though it was barrels of such.

We sat at dinner with Feather and Stacy Truman, a musician in her own right and they were running song ideas past each other. She was the reason he did the punk album, and they'd been dating ever since. Feather didn't talk about her around us, but it was obvious he was madly in love. She was definitely Feather's type, brunette and dreaded. Hell, Stacy dressed and acted like a dirtier hippy than Feather. She'd obviously grown out of her punk phase, and I assume that was Ethan's doing (with a little help of some psertain psubstances, of course).

The gastropub we were eating at was playing news on the tv and a couple clips were played of musicians walking in and out of Bill's studio. That many huge stars attracted a lot of attention, and brought about mystery, given that no details had been released about what was going on. Nobody had known what was going to happen besides Feather until recording started, and now the only people who knew what was happening in that studio were all the artists on the album.

When Feather, Stacy, Amy, and I left, we were swarmed by paparazzi, but we simply kept walking and pushed our way through. Nobody answering any questions until one nervous guy in the back just asked us the simple question of, "What's the album about?"

"Peace, love, unity," answered Feather after stopping to answer the man's question.

We got in our respective cars and returned to our respective houses. Amy and I slept like rocks that night. The next day I got her up bright and early to take her out surfing again, something she had grown to really like despite its somewhat dangerous nature. Her

149

and I showed up to the second day of recording with wet hair and salt on our skin, which made Drew and Laura noticeably jealous. The two of them were too busy between acting, modeling, and now recording this album to surf. I believe at the time Laura hadn't been out since first day of our last tour. It was obvious it was eating her alive.

Meanwhile, Feather sat in a room with Paul, Tom, Robert, and Keith, and I could tell they were all writing a song by the racket they were making. Stacy and I did a cover of "California Dreaming" and Amy sang it with us. I realized that there were only twelve artists if you counted bands as a single people: us, Keith Richards, Paul McCartney, Tom Morello, Robert Plant, Bob Weir arrived that day with the rest of Dead and Company, Brushy, Rome, Stacy, three different street performers, and Dispatch. Feather was counting Amy as an artist and I explained that to her.

We went in with her and we covered the song "Can't Take My Eyes Off You", on my request. Amy thought it was as cheesy as I thought it was cute, as it was one of "our songs". Despite how much she hated being that couple, I could tell she secretly loved doing it as much as I did.

She sang the verses and I took the chorus and played guitar for it. When we got back into the fray of artists, Feather and friends had watched it and greeted us with a bunch of sarcastic "aws", which made us blush, but it really was my favorite song to do for the whole album.

We finished on the third day with Dead and Company playing "Ripple", the three street performers recording "Rock 'n' Roll Suicide", and then I finished it all up by doing "American Pie" with Feather and Tom Morello. Feather had us stay in the booth and the other artists all came in. It was hot, sweaty, and cramped when Feather laid down the first verse of the final song to no instrumental. Drew and Laura gave a beat, and the other artists started playing. Eventually we were all playing and singing.

Feather, Paul, Robert, and Bob switched singing the verses, and all of us on instruments played together, but each person got a solo when they felt one come on. Then, on the very last chorus, we all sang in unison and ended the song.

Billy mixed everything and the album came out sounding real good. We put it up for five dollars an album on iTunes and the Barefoot Studio website (Billy finally made his company official and planned to sign three new artists in the next two years). Within hours of its release, every news site was talking about "Change". By the time I'd woken up the next morning, just over a million copies had been purchased worldwide, and that was more than enough to cover the group's expenses for getting to Standing Rock. It was December at this time, and a group of veterans were supposed to arrive on the same day we were.

Feather spent the remainder of the two weeks preparing for the trek. He got a lot of cold weather clothes, a few, very sturdy tents designed for the harshest of weather, and then a whole lot of food and supplies for the camp.

With my time, I took Amy to Disneyland on a big four night stay in one of the nicest suites at a hotel smack dab in the middle of California Adventure. The park was decorated for Christmas and looked gorgeous. There were more bright and colorful lights than ever before. One of the nights I did a smallish dose of MDMA without Amy knowing, the first time I'd really done any drugs for a long while.

I then did what any sensible person on lots of drugs in Disneyland would do, and I bought a whip and hat outside the Indiana Jones ride, before I cut up to the front with Amy. I did what I normally did in that sort of situation and acted like somebody up front was waiting for me, until I got to the front. At this point in my life, everybody knew me, so when I looked the man with normal sized pupils in the eyes and asked to get get on the ride, he had no problem with letting us on.

Every up down, swirl, and twirl made my whole world whirl. The roaring ride was rickety, but the shit I saw on it was more than just righteous. I became Indy. I was Indy. Every facet of Indiana Jones was me, and I acted as such until we got to Tarzan's treehouse. Now my time as Emperor of Expeditions had ended, but my time as king of the jungle began.

Just before I went to leap from the tree onto a vine, I remembered that I was, in fact, on MDMA and couldn't do anything to sporadic. Amy had no idea what I'd done, and most likely would be pretty pissed if she found out I not only was doing drugs, but that I was doing them at Disneyland. So, I resisted the urge to do as the king of the jungle would do, and continued onto the jungle cruise, where I saw animals I had no idea were native to California!

We finished up with rides for the day, and it was time to continue on with the night. Pure feelings of euphoria washed over me the entire night and I was more uplifted than ever. The energy boost was needed more than ever, as the day in Disneyland had wiped me out, but the MDMA washed away the tiredness. It sprayed it right off my face with a pressure hose of energy and blasted me into alertness. Amy noticed I was finally happy and energetic, as I'd been content, mellow, and a bit depressed until today, and I was acting how I did before I met her. I decided to go and live like a crazy rockstar while I still had a chance to, and that's what tonight was.

I knew Standing Rock was going to change a lot of things. I had lived like I was sixteen for a very long time, but I would have to be somebody for something bigger than myself whether I liked it or not, which I didn't. Skip had the right idea about life, but it was far too late for backsies now. Things were going to change in a way I couldn't imagine, but tonight was a night for fun.

I explained my situation and the influences I was under to Amy, and, to my surprise, she wasn't mad at all. In fact, she wanted the remainder of what I had, so we went and got giant lemonades and turned them into something much more fun. I upped my dose to trip harder and she took a smallish dose, as Amy was not the dirty hippy I was and found herself very unfamiliar with psychedelics of any kind (if we can even call this a true psychedelic, as a good time is almost guaranteed and you don't really blast off).

While she was coming up, we spent a long time sitting on a bench, looking out onto a pond and talked and talked. The future was uncertain, but she repeatedly assured me that she would be apart of it, which was the only true comfort I had. I knew Feather intended me to be a leader, but that was something I didn't want. The responsibility, the potential danger, and the unknown. For the first time since my shroom

153

trip oh so long ago, Fear began to sink its claws in me once more. I looked Amy in the eyes, and before it had a true hold on me, I felt pure love and nothing else. It wasn't just love for Amy, love for this place, or love for this world, it was pure love for everything in existence and existence itself. Love for the good, love for the evil, and love for everything in between. Now I knew when the time would come, I'd be ready to stand beside Feather in whatever was to follow.

It was when we were floating down a canal surrounded by pirates that I realized we had dinner reservations in 20 minutes. Thankfully it was at the restaurant attached to the ride, so when we got off we rushed into the restaurant after smoking a small joint I'd rolled to bring our appetites back.

We were giggling and giddy when we entered. It had been probably around a year since the last time I smoked, and I was "shlit as balls" as Drew and I used to say. At first I was paranoid as all hell, but then I realized I was famous as shit and it didn't matter. Famous people always got to do whatever they wanted, so stopped trying to hold Brian back and let him do his thing.

Thankfully for Brian he made me realize the severity of the situation. We were sitting in a patio while the town our restaurant was in was being raided by pirates. I explained this to Amy but she was convinced it "just wasn't real, that's all part of the ride" and that I was "just tripping", but I knew better.

I had the host sit us down as far away from the pirates as possible, and when one wouldn't stop turning to look at us (rhythmically so I might add, almost as if it was on a timer), I threw my bread across the restaurant at it. Apparently the waiter was a goddamn pirate sympathizer who didn't understand that these people were rapists, looters, and murderers. For some reason, he patronized me while talking to me. Him and Amy laughed at how seriously I was taking everything, but this was no time for games. I hope this waiter realized he wasn't getting any sort of tip, and, if he glanced at Amy's chest again, he would be getting a cutlass to his chest in place of a fifty.

It was when the waiter left and I saw Amy's smile that I remembered the pirates were, in fact, dope as shit. Bran the Black they called me a long time ago. I was the greatest pirate captain who ever sailed the seven seas. None could match my tactical brilliance, or my alcohol tolerance. Looking around I realized my crew was under some voodoo spell that turned them into robots, so I began to hatch a plan.

I realized that the fake pirates needed a real one to lead them to life. I got up to "go to the bathroom." I snuck up to a pirate on the other side of a bridge, and I tried releasing him from his bonds before somebody ran up and ordered me to stop. I explained to them I was getting together a new crew. There was a convoy headed for Tortuga tomorrow and I needed some more money for prostitutes and repairs on my ship that I could easily steal from those British pricks.

It was there that my whole world was shattered. Everything I knew, my whole past, my entire life as the greatest pirate captain to ever sail, was shattered.

Thankfully the worker who I explained my situation to was a big fan of The Bums. I remembered I was a rockstar, and I realized I was tripping. He led me back to the table Amy was at and she died of laughter upon my return.

I came back to reality and began to come down. I apologized to the worker before the waiter came and I ordered jambalaya, gumbo, and told him to make at least 4 po boys. My old foe, the munchies, had returned with a vengeance. It was me versus them once again. It'd been at least a year since they last attacked, and I was determined to conquer them.

After pleasant conversation and contemplation on when and if I'd propose that night or wait. Standing Rock was on the horizon, and that'd be too much stress for either of us to deal with. Plus, we were both rolling and high, and this was something I needed to do sober as the day I was born.

After deciding to wait, I moved onto the more important thing: the void to be vanquished within my stomach. I did what I could to push that void back with a ridiculous amount of food. I shmacked the gumbo and jambalaya in 20 minutes before noticing somebody at another table filming me. I waved at said person before eating the first two po boys and I finally felt the pit in my stomach fill, the forces of darkness were being pushed back to the foul depths from which they came as I suffocated them in delicious Cajun food.

Amy sat in amazement as I turned the remaining two po boys into one and ate the whole thing in less than ten minutes. The entire restaurant stared as I looked at the waiter, and signaled for the check with a smile. The man who was standing in awe at the great feat of food he just witnessed walked over like a zombie and handed me the check, and I handed him a wad of cash and had him keep the change.

We left for Standing Rock the day our stay was up, but not before a food challenge in my honor was created and buying Amy a giant mickey mouse, and stealing myself one of the costumes. After procuring a goofy costume, I was video taped by Drew (who came on the last day), skating around Disneyland before the security tackled me and I was escorted out. Just in time too, otherwise I would've missed my flight. We sent the footage to one of Feather's friends who was working with a professional snowboarder on a stunt show.

Can't You Hear Me
Knockin'

The camp was surrounded by the barren hills of North Dakota. We stayed in the main camp where all the other visitors resided and built a small stage behind it. Generators and solar panels were setup for the speakers. None of the stars accompanying us were staying past our performance except Tom Morello and the street performers.

Two hours before our arrival, a large group of veterans had arrived at the camp. They were eager to hear the concert, but more so to march on the oil loving bastards.

Drew, Laura, and I marched in the front line. Bob and the older artists were at the back of the group since the weather was awful, and getting pepper sprayed, shot with rubber bullets, and being older in a harsh climate was not a good mixture. John Mayer, Tom Morello, and the street performers accompanied us up front. Feather stood about five feet ahead of the whole group and walked alongside the chiefs.

We linked arms with each other, and the other protestors followed. Within seconds we had rows of people linking arms, making an impenetrable human wall. Alone we were weak. Together we were unbreakable.

We made it to a bridge where we faced off with

the police officers, private security, and mercenaries that the company had hired. The officers made a riot shield wall, and they were ready to repel us if we moved further forward. The mercenaries stepped forward to release dogs onto us, and then began shooting rubber bullets about thirty minutes into the standoff. When one person fell, another from behind would step in and replace them until the veterans, dressed in uniform, stepped forward. Alone we were weak. Together we were unbreakable.

The police broke their shield walls, and some of the mercenaries dropped their weapons, many being veterans themselves. The opposition began falling apart, and some began crossing the thirty feet of empty space between us and them to join our ranks. Feather and the chiefs remained in the center where each deserter joined them. Eventually there was a circle of around 30 in the middle of the field. The enemy was losing numbers fast. Alone we were weak. Together we were unbreakable.

Half the cops had left the lines, a good three quarters of the mercenaries stood down, but the remaining ones threw all they had at us. The private security seemed to have no empathy and remained unified. Tear gas, rubber bullets relentlessly rained down, and dogs were running through our ranks before the protestors in the back started wrestling the dogs down and putting muzzles on them. Alone we were weak. Together we were unbreakable.

I was hit by a truck in my side and fell to the ground. I laid on the ground, gasping for air when Drew's hand reached down. Once on my feet, the feeling of a heavily bruised, likely broken rib sent unbearable pain throughout my whole body. With

159

Drew and Laura's assistance, I kept on my feet. Alone we were weak. Together we were unbreakable.

I saw Amy helping load the wounded on stretchers as they were carried couple hundred yards back to the medical tents. She'd seen me go down and I could tell how worried she was, but I shot her a look of reassurance (although the grimace at turning my body most likely made her fear grow).

Feather and the chiefs stood up. His nose was bleeding and his eyes were red and puffy from the pepper spray, but he wasn't phased in the least bit. A fire burned behind his eyes I hadn't seen before, and when I looked into that fire I finally read his thoughts.

Ethan began to chant the chorus of "I Won't Back Down", by Johnny Cash, and soon the entire group of 400 people joined in. Feather, the chiefs, and the deserters linked arms and lead a march on our remaining adversaries.

Fear was in the eys of our foes. They were running low on rubber bullets, and stood at a small squad of around 40 private security officers, 15 mercenaries, and 12 cops.

They laid down their weapons, some of the heads of the DAPL project came via helicopter and met with the chiefs, a meeting that Feather and the leader of the group of veterans were invited to. The pipeline was to be rerouted so that it wouldn't contaminate the water source that was of great importance to the tribe.

That was not enough. Trump remained in office, this pipeline was still to be built, and we were on the brink of a second Vietnam, yet it could be much worst this time. The battle had been won, but the war had just begun.

We played our concert, which received a massive amount of media coverage that raised awareness for the cause, and soon camps were popping up at various sites along the pipeline across the country demanding the pipeline would go unused, and that's what happened. A giant force of 2000 protestors who organized online stood outside the white house before the president and his cabinet bent to their demands that the pipeline be deconstructed and the nation worked to be zero emissions within the next six years.

Despite the accomplishment of getting the pipeline construction to end, the tribes wanted to keep the camp. In later years it would be seen as the headquarters of the Green Army. We stayed with them for a another three weeks. The band pitched together to buy lots of food and building supplies, as well as farming tools to set up a permanent community.

In addition to buying food for the camp, we accompanied the hunters. Since the buffalo had been wiped out in the area, all there was to be had for game were small rabbits and the occasional buck, so they needed all the help they could get. To cover more ground, we hunted from horseback, and to keep with tradition, we only used bows. Never before had I ridden a horse, but I instantly loved it and spent most of the remaining time in the camp mastering the art until a blizzard came and the weather became to harsh to continue to do so.

The veterans wanted to go north to Flint to get the government to do something about the water quality there that was still awful, and that they did. Two weeks after arriving and organizing more protests, the tap water was drinkable and efforts were made across America to improve everybody's water. Hell, they even

161

stopped putting fluoride in after admitting it did more harm to a human's body than good (finally, we caught up with every other first world country who doesn't include fluoride in their water anymore).

I eventually left Feather and all the protests he went to, so that I could go to my place in New York to celebrate Christmas and New Years with Amy. From there, Feather headed back to LA and got in the Travelin' Trouble Machine accompanied by his "generals" for the Peace Army. I started riding horses and only kept up with what Feather was doing through the occasional email, letter, or simply by watching the news before finally deciding to go and join him.

I met them outside a CNN building in the LA area. Since then, most of CNN's executives have stepped down and what they cover on the news changed drastically. They went from being a bitch for the corporate controlled Democrats, to being a real news station showing real news, exposing corruption, and bringing the people the information they needed.

Everything had been peaceful, no riots, and due to new legislation in California and 12 other states, the Peace Army hadn't been brutalized like we were in North Dakota, but then we went to New York. It was to protest the banks who were on the brink of causing another stock crash and a recession worst than the one back in 2008.

We went across country in a huge caravan of cars (though most of Feather's Peace Army, including myself, took planes and met up with the others when they arrived a few days later). Upon arrival to New York, the numbers grew to more than seven and a half thousand protestors, and we marched on Wall Street.

I found myself standing beside Feather as we marched. Thousands were behind us. People broke off and started spray painting the buildings on Wall Street, we held signs, and everybody chanted in unison down the empty street. We stopped to hold just outside of the Goldman Sachs building where private security and police officers waited to meet us, but, unlike in North Dakota, we were prepared for whatever they were going to shoot at us. The front three lines wore gear for football, hockey, and lacrosse.

The rubber bullets came first, and people in the back began to fall left and right, along with those directly hit in the front. Thats when the tower shields were passed up front. The entire time the caravan had been headed East, Feather had commissioned the construction of a hundred and fifty steel shields by various metalworkers in the city.

We created a shield wall like the one we'd seen in Standing Rock, and advanced on the line of officers. Their rubber bullets proved useless, and when the tear gas started coming down, we put on our gas masks and kept marching. Those who didn't have any fell to the ground in pain or ran to the hills. The opposition began angling their weapons upwards to hit the unprotected protestors behind us. A hundred or so riot officers began firing their rubber bullets into the air. Most of the people behind us began to disperse as projectiles rained down and tear gas filled their lungs and eyes, but some broke off and began to riot, something we'd repeatedly said not to do.

Only myself, Feather, and a hundred armored protestors remained at the front. The others fell back a few hundred yards and kept protesting. Our lightly armored line of hippies was the only thing between people exercising their constitutional right and those being paid by the ones trying to take those away.

There was at least a hundred fifty riot control officers facing us 40 yards away. I knew more were bound to come from the sound of bricks shattering windows, people vandalizing the office buildings, and the sight of complete chaos behind me. Two hundred or so people were rioting, but thousands were peacefully protesting.

The chaos wasn't what we wanted   Faces lacking familiarity were the ones defying command and it was destruction they did demand. A group of people were beating a security officer to get into one of the buildings, and I realized those faces were, in fact, familiar.   They were the mercenaries and private security from Standing Rock. Feather saw it too, so he fell behind me.

I grabbed his shield to keep him protected while he sent out a the lesser commanders who were with the protestors.   He made them aware of the situation, and the protestors who'd fled returned and began fighting with the rioters.

When the first few hundred rioters were attacked, it was obvious that 2,500 of our 7,000 had been bought by the enemy. Complete and utter chaos broke out, and Wall Street was turned into a battleground.   The riot officers we faced were noticeably confused, but not for long. Their cavalry had arrived.

Mounted officers charged us. Our shield wall stood no chance against the officers on horseback. On the first charge, a quarter of those who stood with us fell.   They were on the ground, unconscious, and possibly lifeless.   What caused it to escalate to this point was unknown to me. All we had been trying to do was protest, but those who had employed the mercenaries were not very happy with us showing up on their doorstep.

The mounted officers came for a second charge, and this time I ran with Feather at my side to meet them. A nightstick connected with Ethan's skull, and he crumpled despite the hard hockey helmet he was wearing. At the same time, I launched my shield, and it connected with the officer's head. He crashed to the ground from his high horse, unmoving. I threw my helmet off and sprinted for the confused and scared horse, jumped on, and charged at the rioters. With a two by four I'd spotted and scooped up near an alley, I started knocking rioters down left and right.

The wall of protestors laid in the street, some with pools of blood around their heads. The other officers chased after me, but I easily evaded them. One charged at me head on with his night stick raised. I knocked the hard, plastic club away before countering and hitting him in the back of the head and he fell. Another came to meet me, and we traded blows for a few seconds more before I climbed from my horse onto his and threw him off.

Next there was a deafening crack, instantly followed by the feeling of a truck slamming into my left shoulder. I fell off the horse and landed on the back of my head. Then there was black.

"Kevin, are you awake?" I heard Amy say. Once again I was in a hospital bed with a throbbing pain in the back of my head, but this time there was a pain unlike any other in my shoulder.

"What happened?" I muttered.

165

"You got shot! What were you thinking Kevin? I saw the news, it was beyond chaos out there, that was fucking war!" Amy exclaimed.

"Somebody hired people to incite a riot, make the protest look bad. There were mounted officers, they took out Feather. Is he okay?"

"He's got a bad concussion, fifty seven protestors died, among them was Stacy. I know her and Feather had broke up before standing rock, but I can't imagine what he's going through right now. So many more are in the hospital, it was complete insanity! It's been all over the news for the past few hours, and after you got shot, it got even worst."

"Do you know who shot me?"

"It was one of the mercenaries. He's being tried for attempted manslaughter and inciting a riot in two weeks. Please, Kevin, no more of this, I'm begging you. This was way too close. If that bullet landed a few more inches down and to the right, you'd be dead. I have no idea what I would do with myself if I had to bury you, Kevin."

"But I'm not dead. Amy, there's so much shit going on. You saw it yourself, this is fucking crazy! This is a war that I helped start, I have to help end it!" I exclaimed as I tried to sit up before laying back down from the excruciating pain.

"Kevin, please. You've been out doing so much, you haven't been home in so long. You've been so consumed by all of this, and goddammit I miss you! I miss my boyfriend. I miss the Kevin who was fun and carefree, the man I loved! Now all you care about are these stupid protests and where you're going to follow Feather into battle next. Let Ethan take care of all this, he doesn't need you for it anymore. Come home, please. If not for yourself, come home for me."

"Amy..."

"Kevin, I'm not asking you to, I'm begging you to come home. You have a choice."

"Amy, please don't do this."

"Kevin, I can't bear to see anything like this happen again, next time you might not be so lucky. Please Kevin, I love you."

"Okay."

"Okay?"

"I'll come home. I'm done with this, with following Feather, unless it's something dire. If Feather really, really needs my help, I have to help him. He's family Amy."

The next few months I spent recuperating and watching the news. I made it to each and every one of Amy's shows, even if I'd already seen her perform the same show twice that week, and her performances were all outstanding. She even won three more Tony's and I was beyond happy for her. Watching her was inspiring, and I did what I knew Feather had been doing. I started writing.

Ethan had left for Ireland after recovering and accepting 4 different Grammy's on behalf of the band. I kept in touch with those he made generals of his Army for Peace and relayed messages from him to them. He published a few books about or centered around Celtic mythology, but one mentioned the Faewilds and a forest king. If only I could've asked him where he got the inspiration for those, as I thought those were places that Brian made up.

Brokedown Palace

A day before he came back, I got a text from Ethan. He told me to turn on the news, and, although I was watching The Big Lebowski with Amy, I switched the TV right away. President Trump had not only declared war, but released the first round of birthdates for the draft. Within hours there were all sorts of notifications being sent to my phone. I was getting private messages left and right on my Reddit account that was used to manage the Peace Army page. All the generals, except for the three that used fake birthdates, had been drafted. There were posts all over. Thousands of people subscribed to the account were being drafted. They had targeted us. Thankfully I wasn't actually born on April 20th, 1969, but Feather had the account for a while and used his real birthday when he signed up.

"What is it? What's wrong?" Amy asked in a panic.

"It's this draft, almost half the protestors got drafted. All the generals of Feather's Peace Army got drafted. Well, all except three and me, who lied about their birthdays on their reddit accounts. Ethan didn't lie. Look right there, on the TV, that's his birthday. They're sending them to die!. Look! there's already peace protestors outside of the capitol building, I have to go," I exclaimed.

"Kevin, please, don't go down to DC," Amy said.

"They're going to need me," I said before

Feather sent me a text reading: *I'll be back in the states tomorrow, I'll drop the TTM off near your penthouse and send you the location. You're going to need it. I'm throwing my phone in a river and tripping tonight, I'll see you after the war.*

"Kevin, they've been doing fine without you. If they really, really need you, go, but please, I need you here."

"I'm gonna have to go. Feather just texted, he's leaving the van out here. He wants it there since he can't show up. All the other protests he's done recently, the van has been on the front line. Wherever that van travels, trouble for assholes follows."

"But I need to see you here, Kevin. It's been so nice finally having you back, you can't just leave now. Hell, you started writing a show! You've done a whole two acts! It looks so good already. Finish that, and we can both go."

"Babe, you saw how dangerous it can be. Are you sure?"

"Yes, Kevin, I'm sure."

I finished the show, and the protests were going well. Nothing big happened beyond the protestors being abused like normal. There was a force of nine thousand camping outside the white house, and another couple hundred sitting outside the capitol building who were pushing congress to impeach Trump. I was still in New York. I finished writing my musical, but the songs I'd came up with were far from the quality I wanted for the show, so I got in contact with a certain somebody by the name of Stephen Sondheim.

The first day he came by, Amy was out getting her hair done before her last show, and when she came home and we were sitting around writing music, she was so happy she cried. It just so happened that day was her birthday as well, so the three of us went out for an outstanding lunch as part of my present for her (alongside expensive jewelry, oversized stuffed animals, and what not).

The diner we went to was excellent, but the news story wasn't. Two days ago multiple US military bases were ambushed, the body count was already in the thousands. Trump was throwing all we had at the Islamic State, and they were responding in the same way. The four sieges that had began were at stalemates, but it looked like we'd end up losing three of the four given that we were far from having the home field advantage.

Amy noticed how I was fidgeting nonstop the whole time. I saw the names of two of Feather's generals who I'd met back in Standing Rock pop up on the list of those killed in action. They were solid guys, one of them newly made into a father. They wanted peace, love, and equality for all, and all they got was a bullet and an orphan.

The news station bugged Feather for an interview, asking him about what he was going to do when he started getting shot at, to which he responded, "I dunno, maybe I'll whip out my dick and spin it around. Might act like a shield! You think if I get hard enough the bullets will bounce off like a blaster bolt on a lightsaber? The fuck kind of question is that? What will I do when I get shot at? Myself and my associates who were purposefully drafted are pacifists you fucks. None of us are firing back. I've told you guys that and I've told three other stations that. But, to answer you're stupid question, I'll probably just play music behind a barrier. Who's gonna shoot the guy in the middle of a jam session? That's just cruel! They didn't let me bring any of my instruments so I made this little thing," and he pulled out what I recognized to be a cigar box guitar. "Now will you guys please fuck off, I'm trying to forget I'm in a warzone."

"Ethan seems to be doing well," Amy joked.

"It's only a matter of time. I know they're trying to break him. He's close, I can tell," I responded, the grave tone of my voice matching the grave tone of the situation.

"I'm sure he'll be fine, Kevin," Sondheim added.

"They drafted him on purpose. He's the biggest threat to the establishment since that one old guy who I remember hearing about a while back. If he doesn't step into line, they're going to make sure he gets shot. I think I'm gonna head home," I finished before getting up and paying for all of our food and marching home by myself.

A week later I'd got a director for my show and just finished sitting through the first auditions. Amy was playing a lead, and some other guy I could give a shit about was too. The rest of the options I left up to the director. I had too much on my mind to focus on who's getting cast in what role. In fact, I decided to leave the rest of the show up to the director, to Amy's disdain. I felt bad because she was looking forward to working with me on a show, but like I said, I had far too much on my mind at the time.

I'd been home for months, but since body counts with lists of names, a good eighth of which I could recognize, showed up nearly every night, I was

171

completely checked out. I smoked for the first time since Disneyland, and I smoked a lot. It was at seven in the evening that Amy came home and woke me up on the couch, a look of disappointment in her eyes and a tint of red in mine.

"Are you high?" she asked.

"Haha, yaaaa man," I responded.

"Oh baby, come here," she said before grabbing me and holding me close to her heart.

I felt comfortable and safe on the outside, but my mind was racing. I convinced myself in a weed-induced panic attack that Feather had just died and broke down into tears. Unable to breathe, I just began to gasp for air. Amy just sat there and did what she could to make me feel better, her touch was the only thing I wanted in that moment. Hell, it was the only reason I even wanted to be alive in that moment. Then, there was a knock. I thought I was hearing things, that the sadness had drove me to insanity. Maybe it was Ethan. Maybe Ethan was back. Maybe I was about to see my brother again.

"Kevin, they need you at the protests," Drew said. His voice had gone unheard by my ears for over a year.

"Drew, it's too dangerous. I could get put back in the hospital, or worst," I responded.

"Damn it Kevin! Ethan, people you're friends with, and so many others are out over seas getting shot at and dying in some shit show of a war that's only happening to take out people opposing that orange faced asshole! They need a leader. Lauralyn and I have been down there for the past week, but they don't listen to us. They're planning a riot. People will die and get hurt, and it's going to end up like Wall Street,

172

but much much worst. The movement is going to lose a lot of credibility. Feather isn't here to calm them. You need to step up," Drew explained.

"No."

"No?"

"No."

"Why the fuck not Kevin?"

"I'm not Ethan goddammit! I'm not a leader! I don't wanna be involved with that mess, and, shit, we both know that if I get active again, I'm gonna be in the same place as Feather when the next round of the draft comes out!"

"Kevin, if you don't want to lead, at least be some sort of voice of reason. They will listen to you. We can't have another Wall Street."

"I told Amy I wouldn't unless they really needed me, and you guys don't."

"Shit Kevin! What happened? I haven't talked to you for over a year! You used to be a fucking rockstar and now you're writing musicals!"

"I'm sorry I didn't decide to become a fucking junkie like you!" I screamed and lifted up his shirt sleeve. Needle scars went up and down Drew's arm.

"Kevin, go. I'll come down and meet you in a few days. You need to go," Amy said after approaching the doorway. She pulled me aside and said, "if the protest doesn't need you, Drew does, Kevin. He knows he does, that's why he's here. Help him, please."

"Okay," I said before grabbing a couple shirts, my guitar, and the rest of the weed I'd bought.

"Do you really need that?" Amy said.

"Might as well get my money's worth. I'll see you in a couple days," I finished before walking out the

173

door.

"How'd you know I was using again?" Drew said.

"Are you kidding me? I knew your dumbass would," I laughed.

"You sounded a lot more pissed off about it five seconds ago."

"Oh, I still am, but I'm gonna take you fishing after the protests, we'll deal with it then, but til that comes, let's get fuckin' baked. I have a surprise for you."

Drew's eyes were wide open when I showed him the Travelin Trouble Machine. There was a group of fans waiting outside it, knowing we had to come by sometime. The two of us signed CDs, rolling papers, asses, and whatever else people wanted to put our signature on. It felt good to be a superstar again, but it felt even better to be sitting shotgun with Drew driving the van. I looked in the back, and Feather's surfboards were there. I really knew why he'd dropped the van off then.

We took the coast down to DC and made a few pit stops at the few good breaks we could find to have much needed surf sessions. I hadn't seen Drew for a while, but it had been even longer since I'd really been in the water. It was hard at first, my shoulder still hurt when I pushed it too hard, but I was able to get a wave. When I dropped in, everything melted. It didn't matter that I didn't have one of my brothers here, that everything we'd built turned to shit the moment we spoke up, or that Drew's entire life was crumbling before my eyes and had been for a while, but I did nothing to stop it. No, none of it mattered for the

174

fifteen seconds that I cruised parallel to the coast. I
paddled back and my gaze met Drew's, we both smiled.
A surf contest like the ones we'd have everyday so long
ago ensued.

It was the night after our last session before
heading inland that I was first exposed to heroin and
true addiction. I could tell Drew was doing what he
could to not use around me by his clammy skin and
constant shaking. As somebody who hates needles
more than anything, the whole process seemed
extremely unappealing. It looked like quite the chore
to heat the product up, put it in a syringe, and then
shoot up.

Drew had a look of relief unlike any I'd ever
seen when he laid back and closed his eyes after he
pushed the poison into his veins.. He just laid there so I
carried him back to the van, put some blankets on him,
and passed the hell out.

When I woke up, Drew was still asleep. I still
can't understand why anybody would use something
that just knocks you out and fucks your body up, but to
each their own, I guess. Upon arriving in DC, it didn't
take long to find the protestors. There were massive
crowds, the numbers given on the news were much
lower than the reality. There was definitely more than
the reported 15,000 people in the street. At least
twenty five thousand protestors populated the asphalt
up and down DC. Hell, the national guard had been
called to contain everybody to a few blocks.

Those few blocks leading up to the white house
were thick with protestors who parted as we
approached, almost all of them recognizing the van and
its occupants. I saw a few groups of people putting

175

sports gear on in anticipation of the riot to happen later that night, but they stopped what they were doing when they saw me. Many of those getting ready to riot were the same ones I stood side by side with on Wall Street, and the look of disapproval I gave them was enough for them to get the message.

Soon we were at the fence, right up next to it. The front bumper of the van touching the black, metal bars. I had no idea what to do, so I thought to myself, *what would Feather do?* And memories of our first concerts flooded back into my head. Impromptu concerts made possible by various acts of trespassing, theft, and occasionally a bit of vandalism. That's when I knew why Feather had left building supplies in the back of the van.

One of the three generals who evaded the draft approached me and notified me that "the materials are ready when you are." At first I didn't know what the materials were, but then I realized that Feather wanted us to build a stage, and I were ready as all hell to do so.

Laura quickly found us when preparations started and gave me a giant hug, tears that were streaming down her face wetted my shirt.

"Aw Laura, I'm glad to see you too," I responded.

"Kevin, Feather is on the front, his platoon is supposed to be deployed for the next siege. They're the first wave of attackers. They're gonna be covering the siege live," Laura said.

"It's Feather, he'll be fine. He'll just keep his head down and make it out okay. He's done a good job of that so far," I explained.

"I don't know, Kevin. They're covering it live and just interviewed him, he seemed so different. He seemed broken," Laura said while on the brink of tears.

"He's not broken. Feather will never let them break him, never let them have the satisfaction of that. Ethan would die before he let's the war break him," I said.

"What do you two exactly mean by Feather breaking?" Drew asked.

"If he killed a man, even if they were shooting at him, he'd be broken," Laura answered. "He swore off violence a long time ago. Hell, he cut his wrists the night he punched the guy in the face that night of our last tour."

"Shit... I bet he'll make it out okay. We're talking about Feather here. Look at what he's done. Look at what's around us. So many years ago, we were just two pairs of surf bums who met at a concert, and he brought us together as friends, and then brought us together as a band. He's gone on and done so much more than that. This is all because of Feather. All these protests, all the change that's happening. He's unified all these people for a single cause: peace, equality, and love. There's nothing more people need in life, and Feather showed the world that. Feather is going to make it back home," I finished.

Three guys came up and said all the pieces of the stage are ready and 60 builders were on standby. I gave the order and we all rushed over the white house fence and dropped the building supplies smack dab in the middle of it. It was a simple stage that we quickly set up, and within seconds, hundreds were rushing over the fence seeing that The Bums were about to have their first concert in years. Security rushed out of the building, shouting with guns raised, but we just got up there and started playing as quickly as possible. When the security started to get close to the stage, the crowd created a human wall. We were encircled on all sides by a sea of people, more and more making it bigger by the second.

We were playing our hearts out and I played Johnny B. Goode in recognition of where I was. The first time I played that song was much different than playing it now. I was comfortable and in my element. Hell, I'd been here before. The crowd was loving it, a few of the security guards were starting to dig it, and we were on top of the world. That's when I saw President Trump for the first time.

He came out of the building and started screaming for us to get down, to quit disrespecting him, and get on with our lives to do something productive. To which I promptly responded with, "We are doing something productive. We're trying to end a war you started because you couldn't take people talking shit. Fuck you Trump, step down or end this war. If Ethan dies, and you're still in office within 24 hours of it, I'll fucking make sure you can go and have a long, long chat with him."

"Well, I hope your bite is as big as your bark, maybe you didn't see the news or somethin'," Trump replied before retreating back into the white house.

I stopped. My whole world shattered, I took out my phone and typed the word "Feather" in, knowing what I would find, but I had to see it to believe it. The first result was a video that looked like some interview. I tapped it and watched.

"So, as you can see, we're here with rockstar turned activist, Ethan Feather, and he's with his platoon pinned down in the streets. How's your day going there, Private Feather?" an interviewer asked through a robot with a camera and speakers mounted to it.

"How the fuck do you think it's going? I thought I told you guys to fuck off!" Feather responded, annoyed and not wanting to talk. Tears began to pour out of my eyes seeing the tortured state of the man I could call a brother, knowing what was coming.

"As a pacifist, what are you to do in a situation like this one, where the only choice is to fight your way out?" the interviewer asked.

"You're here, interviewing a guy on the front lines, of a FUCKING WAR, from behind the safety of a robot! You're here, asking a guy drafted only because he opposed the FUCKING IDIOT in office because that guy just wanted to be able to live in a place without some racist, rich fucks pulling the strings, fucking over everybody and everything, even the very planet we live on, just so they can get richer! How much money do you really need? I'm here and I've got what, 40 million or so throughout my life, and I donated almost all of it because that's more money than I know what to do with! Trump and his cabinet sit around and talk about who they'll fuck next, what they'll fuck next, and all for the sake of getting more money. They don't do anything with that money, it just sits there and it's worthless. The street performer with twenty bucks and a moldy sandwich is worth just as much as the multi-billionaire sitting in a mansion, trading emails with congresspeople on how much money he'll give them for the next war they start! Hell, that performer is worth twenty times more since he has a fucking soul! Money is meaningless. Power is meaningless. That's what this war is about, so this war is fucking meaningless. I'm not gonna take a single life because some fucking idiot

179

wants me to!" Feather screamed and shouted at the interviewer. In that moment there was more emotion behind his voice than I'd ever heard before. Then, gunshots started ringing out, and Feather dropped his weapon, took of his vest, took off his boots, and took off his shirt. He was in nothing but his camo pants when he took out a joint and lit it up and nodded to the camera with a smile on his face.

Then, he stood up, spread out his arms and blood sprayed everywhere. Next, his lifeless, bullet riddled body fell next to the camera and the joint fell out onto the ground and into a puddle. The rest of his platoon followed suit along the wall, and I assumed the other soldiers in the area did as well with the screams of pain that could be heard throughout. The gunshots stopped, and so did the video.

I dropped my phone and collapsed to my knees. There, in front of thousands upon thousands of people, I cried. The people I was supposed to lead, those who were looking to me for direction now that Feather was gone for good, I just stood there and I cried. I saw news crews over the fence with their cameras aimed at me, most likely zoomed in on my tears. The only thing that got more ratings than bloodshed were the tears that followed, and my tears were joined by those of everybody's in the crowd. We were supposed to at least seem somewhat threatening, but there we were, weeping for Ethan.

I got a text from Amy and nine times out of ten, I would've immediately responded, but this time, I just threw my phone on the ground and it skidded across the stage. Laura was sitting there, she looked emotionless, blank, like all the life had been sucked out of her. Drew was rubbing his finger on his gums, and I was jealous of him. I wanted to go numb, but for the first time in a while, I was really, truly feeling. So I played, and I played and I played. A minute went by on my knees, then ten more on my feet, and then I dropped the guitar.

I thought back to the album we recorded in what felt like a lifetime ago, the one that the protests, and I now knew why Feather had us sing the song we did. I dropped my guitar on the ground, it was too heavy to hold. I knew that somewhere inside the house behind me, Trump was feeling as though he won because Feather was dead, and so was everybody there on his side. I was out to prove him wrong.

I started singing "Ain't No Grave", my voice shook and quivered, but the crowd quickly started to join in. Soon people were coming up onto stage, and we kept singing. I couldn't see him, but I knew Trump could hear us, all of us. There was at least 3000, and unlike Wall Street, we were unified. I saw some of the mercenaries, but they weren't there to incite a riot, they were there to stand by us against Trump.

We were clapping and stomping and then I stepped down from the stage. Hundreds more filed in and joined the mob, some hadn't even been apart of the protests to begin with. People from all over the country who had come because Feather had told them to so long ago. People who came because they saw it on the news. People who came because they saw the massive crowd and wanted to figure out what was going on. People were there because they just knew being there was what they had to do.

I began to walk, I reached a steady pace and the people fell in behind me. I got to the white house doors and the whole crowd was still chanting. The doors were locked, so I found a rock and threw it through the window. The security began to fire shots into the crowd, and, despite the bodies on the ground, people rushed in through the opening and overcame the security within seconds.

The doors opened and I walked through, and at this point the secret service gave up trying to stop us, in fact, more than half of those present joined us. Workers in the white house: servants, chefs, maids, and whoever else was there joined us. Trump had locked himself in the oval office upon hearing the commotion, but we quickly took the doors down. I took out my phone and started filming, and just before I was about to speak up, Laura butted in.

"Hey asshole, your time is up. You do not represent the people, so the people ask you to step down. Look around you, everybody here wants you out, even you own damn secret service. Racism, bigotry, and hatred will reign no longer. You will reign no longer. Resign and leave now, or we will forcibly remove you from office, whether you're alive or not, I could give a shit, but you will step down and you'll do it now, Mr. President," Laura explained, hatred in her eyes, something I hadn't seen in them ever before.

Trump sat there, astonished, unable to believe what was going on. I saw him pinch himself and look up again, and this time with a look of terror unmatched by any I'd ever seen before. Trump looked at the camera I had on my phone, and he resigned as president before walking out. The crowd parted for him, but not to give him safe passage, so that people could spit on him. I assume that Trump was drenched by the time he got to whatever car or limo was there to pick him up. He was gonna head home, get his suit cleaned, hopefully off himself, and his friends would be scared, for a while at least. We'd finally won our first battle, and the tide was turning, but I had no idea how long things would move in our favor. I was in this for Feather, and now I'd avenged him. Somebody who knew what they were doing would take my place, and I would be able to go home, and put this shit behind me.

I left the ruined White House as soon as I could, and I climbed on top of the white house to sit. Drew joined me, and we gazed out onto the endless world that spanned before us.

Apollo and Artemis were staring across the earth at each other while the sun and moon stood in perfect balance. They came to see if Feather was truly gone, but Trump was too. Laura came and sat down to observe the time of balance with us. There was a crowd down below us, celebrating the accomplishment, but we weren't. That guy Feather, he was dead.

CITY OF STARS

Feather's actual funeral was small, but there were vigils across the nation. We had it in San Francisco, and it was a closed casket. I was the only one who saw his nearly unrecognizable, bullet riddled body. I couldn't believe that it was really him. I still can't. That guy Feather was dead and still is.

I spent the next four years in New York with Amy, expecting Feather to walk in our apartment with a crazy idea that would take us on another magnificent adventure. He never showed up.

We got married on Ethan's birthday four months following his death. The wedding was as small as the funeral. Only a few of Amy's family members and friends showing up for her. Skip, Erin, Drew, and Laura were the only ones there for me. Between Drew and Laura there was an empty seat. That way when Feather was going to barge in and say it was all a joke he'd know exactly where to sit. He never did.

I hadn't seen my bandmates since Feather's funeral, and we didn't spend much time catching up. The only person I really talked to at the wedding was Skip. There he explained to me that in a few years, he wanted to retire. I'd already bought a house down in Baja that Feather and I were supposed to go retire to with our families where we'd raise them beach bum style. I knew that Skip would go and live there as a way for me to "pay him back for raising me".

Coco was old and lazy, depressed as I was. I spent most of my time just sitting around the penthouse with that pup, writing plays, musicals, and various stories. I hadn't touched a guitar since the day that Feather had died.

"Kevin, you're not healthy, I'm going to retire from Broadway," Amy told me one night after we got back from the Tony's (of which she'd won fourteen of at this point in her career).

"Princess, you don't have to. You love Broadway, you don't have to do that for me," I responded, barely managing to crack a fake smile.

"Drew shaped up and moved on. You know he's 3 years clean now?"

"Is he?"

"Kevin, we're going to sell the penthouse. Skip wants you to take over."

"The shop?"

"Yes. We've been texting, he's worried. Skip wanted to retire years ago, Kevin, but you've been stuck. He told me that you were never meant to be a rockstar, you were supposed to be a beach bum," Amy joked before walking away.

We left New York City two weeks later and that's how I got to this point. I've been running the shop for almost a year now, Laura has been acting, and Drew became a priest. Skip was right, I wasn't happy. I could only be happy when I took Amy out surfing, or when we had a beach barbecue with our neighbors, Coco, and our new rottweiler, Casey. I started giving free guitar lessons every Sunday, and, despite pressure from the fanbase of The Bums, I never released another song. I jammed when I was sitting around the shop and started doing the whole freestyle singing thing Feather was so fond of. Every once in a while I go to a bar and

I'll play, but that's just for fun and free drinks. I have plans to hike the Pacific Crest Trail, something Feather and I occasionally talked about, and I'm hoping to be ready in the next two years.

An actor-turned-governor of California who threatened to secede during the Trump reign became president, but I could care less. If there was one thing I'd learned, it's that politics are beyond bullshit. No matter what happens, you can always just keep living your life in a place like this. There'll always be an Ethan out there who can rally the people, so that people like me can sit back and have a beer on the beach.

All the music of the Bums was free on our website, and I occasionally played a song or two of ours for a fan who went out of their way to find me (something I made sure was hard to do). I didn't need any more money. Hell, I'd used most of it to help set up marine preserves. What I needed, I had; Amy, my dogs, the shop, and little Ethan Douglas was on the way.

I was finally happy.

www.ingramcontent.com/pod-product-compliance
Lightning Source LLC
Chambersburg PA
CBHW022111170626

46808CB00002B/692